TEG'S 1994

AN ANTICIPATION OF
THE NEAR FUTURE

BOOKS BY ROBERT THEOBALD

The Rich and the Poor (1960)
The Challenge of Abundance (1961)
Profit Potential in the Developing Countries (1962)
Free Men and Free Markets (1963)
Business Potential in the European Common Market (1963)
The Guaranteed Income, ed. (1966)
Social Policies for America in the Seventies, ed. (1968)
Committed Spending: A Route to Economic Security, ed. (1968)
An Alternative Future for America II (1970)
The Economics of Abundance (1970)
Bobbs-Merrill Dialogue Series, ed.
Habit and Habitat (1972)
Futures Conditional (1972)

TEG'S 1994

AN ANTICIPATION OF
THE NEAR FUTURE

ROBERT THEOBALD
AND
J. M. SCOTT

THE SWALLOW PRESS INC.
CHICAGO

Published by
The Swallow Press Incorporated
1139 South Wabash Avenue
Chicago, Illinois 60605

ISBN (cloth) 0-8040-0509-5
ISBN (paper) 0-8040-0510-9
LIBRARY OF CONGRESS CATALOG NO. 70-150754

This book is printed on 100% recycled paper.

Permission is not required for quotations of up to 500 words. Those quoting, however, should identify the character advancing the views cited and add the following statement to the normal acknowledgment note:

The ideas expressed by this character should not be assumed to reflect the views of the authors.

DEDICATION

This book is lovingly dedicated to our nieces, nephews and god-children: *William, Martin, Niall, Anita Naoko, Vanessa, Rachel Ada, Paul Francis, Carol Anne, Alexander, Daniella Abigail, Fiona, Ra'anan;* who are Teg's contemporaries and will be contributing their personalities and their work to their communities in the world of 1994.

We hope to be able to assist them in whatever they decide to do.

CONTENTS

INTRODUCTION

As we approach the fourth quarter of our century, ecological awareness is becoming generalized. The implications of this new attitude go far beyond the obvious. Manifestly, there is already a new environmental aesthetic, a reconceptualization of use and waste, of surplus and sufficiency. There is also emerging a new relationship between man and ecology; man lives *with* the land, not from it. Man's physical surroundings are no longer regarded as a scene to be surveyed from outside the picture. The nineteenth century ego portrait of nature tamed in the background has become a landscape with figures and system-structures: the viewer has become participant.

Three years ago, at the time *Teg's 1994* was at the organization stage, the ecological re-emphasis was already apparent. We felt that this re-emphasis was potentially applicable to communication relationships other than man / ecology. In some areas, such as the theatre, where audience involvement was increasing, the new participant communication was already taking place. The way in which *Teg's 1994* is organized is our attempt to apply the viewer-as-participant principle to print. This is a participation book.

Some customary reader assumptions about books therefore do not hold true for *Teg's.* First, we are not writing as authors to a public, with an implied one-to-one relationship between writer and reader. Rather, we ask you to remain aware while reading that these printed pages are a focus for communication among a group of people interested in the future. A multi-directional communication is already in process; we began by a request for reader participation in the mimeographed edition of *Teg's 1994* sent out in 1969 / 1970. Reader response to us is printed at the back of this volume; readers also communicated directly with each other, or held discussion groups. Our response to readers is printed immediately following the readers' responses to us. We invite all of you to continue this process by communicating with each other and with us: the blank column on each page is provided for your initial participation as you read.

Second, this is a participant book on the future and it therefore differs from other future-books on many levels other than organization. It is essential that the reader does not assume that this is any of the familiar types of "futurist" books. Futurist authors, in the social or related sciences, commonly assume that in order to proceed into the future it is only necessary to have an understanding of industrial-era realities, which, they assume, represent the present. Science-fiction authors, theoretically less limited in approach and goals, nevertheless frequently restrict themselves to working out the impact of minor changes in industrial-era styles rather than exploring imaginatively the effects of a profound cultural and material reorganization.

A third incorrect, if reasonable, assumption would be that the description of events represents our own ideal view of the future. It very definitely does not. In our opinion, Teg's world would make a very poor Utopia for anybody. The twenty-five-year period described in *Teg's 1994* begins in the late sixties; the events described are one possible series of workings-out of tendencies already apparent at that time. *Teg's 1994* is neither the best way these tendencies could be worked out, nor the worst—it is simply the least intolerable that we can imagine *without there having been a fundamental and immediate change in trends already apparent.*

Teg and her contemporaries live in an era of full communications, with its own problem/possibilities. They are different from those of the industrial era, with which we are so familiar. The thoughts and actions of the protagonists relate to the communications world. The reader may, therefore, find it helpful to imagine himself in such a world, as a participant, not as a viewer, before beginning the book. Perhaps the reader's imagined communication world may be different in degree or kind from that outline in *Teg's 1994.* In this sense the book can be used as a Rorschach test, revealing to the reader his own ideas about the future.

* * *   * * *   * * *

Whatever one's personal view of the future, it is clear that communications will play a major part. The speeding up of the idea-development process means the reorganizing of society. At the present time we are not accustomed to fast idea-development; rather, we are becoming used to fast data communication and processing. This is an industrial-era technique with an industrial product. In effect, we are told how to proceed in any given situation along lines which have already been followed.

It is necessary to distinguish clearly between ideas and data. Data is used to plot the steps which must be taken in order to most effectively fulfill the goals already agreed upon by the society. Thus, for example, the unemployment rate today serves as an indicator of the divergence between the present situation and the desired situation. A high level of unemployment is considered unfavorable at the present time and the society, in general, agrees that it is desirable to reduce unemployment unless other goals are more urgent. Data about the unemployment situation is, therefore, used in a particular way because the society generally shares the goal of full employment. The same data would be used very differently if the society believed that its appropriate long-range goal were full *un*employment rather than full employment.

What is the nature of the shift from the industrial era to the communications era? The main goals of the late industrial era were the maximum rate of economic growth and distribution of resources through full employment. Until very recently, it was generally assumed that these goals would continue to be valid for an indefinite time into the future, both in America and throughout the world. Today there is growing agreement that the main goals of the late industrial era are inappropriate to present conditions. Mankind is now beginning to try to discover the idea-structures which are relevant to the new conditions which man's success has created.

John Maynard Keynes, the British economist, argued that "In the long run, it is ideas and not men which rule the world." Ideas determine the way in which people perceive their world and the actions which they believe to be in their self-interest. When idea-structures change, so do definitions of individual and societal self-interest. For example, existing differences in idea-structures explain why many of the young are proposing different policies to deal with national and world problem/possibilities, as compared to many of those who now hold positions of structural authority.

As man's power increases, the effects of his actions become more and more far-reaching and the secondary and tertiary consequences so significant that they can no longer be ignored. We have, therefore, reached the point where we must choose new processes appropriate for the communications era. We are confronted with the necessity for choice. Our present institutions were not designed for this purpose. Choice will only be possible within a new idea-structure, one which is based on systemic rather than linear thinking.

One of the unexpected consequences of the shift from linear to systemic thinking is that the shortest distance between two points ceases to be the "direct route": one is forced to think in oblique, indirect terms. (In chess this pattern is called "Knight's move.") In addition, while linear thinking can occur within a competitive society, systemic thinking requires a cooperative society. Systemic thinking involves such a wide range of skills that only cooperation between all those with the necessary knowledge can be adequate to study problem/possibilities.

In effect, we are engaged in a shift from the concept of "growth" to the concept of process—the creation of new patterns. One of our most urgent tasks is to discover the implications of the change in idea-structures from growth to process.

If we are to understand this issue, we must keep the distinction between idea-structures and data clearly in mind. Until we have developed a *new set* of ideas on which new processes can be based, the significance of any piece of data for decision-making cannot be evaluated. We cannot tell whether a rapid rise in GNP is good or bad, whether a high birth rate is useful or dangerous, whether "unemployment" should be avoided or encouraged unless we know what idea-structures are appropriate to present realities and what purposes are implied by these idea-structures.

The task we must carry through in the immediate future is therefore totally different from that which our present institutions were designed to accomplish. Until we began to perceive the need for a profound shift in idea-structures, we were properly occupied as individuals and nations with the fulfillment of already-known goals. Now that we are becoming aware that we must change our idea-structures, and with them our processes, we are confronted with a different challenge. The challenge is to create a different pattern of societal organization: in effect, a new culture.

* * *   * * *   * * *

How do idea-structures change? This is a question to which we are only now finding the answers. We do, however, already possess far more knowledge on this subject than is generally recognized. We know that idea-structures do not change because new data emerges. New data may convince people that the strategy and tactics presently employed to meet goals are ineffective. Data alone, however, will not change idea-structures.

A startling case of this reality is now emerging in the field of ecology, environment, and economic policy. An increasing number of people are aware that there is a direct correlation between economic growth and pollution. However, rather than reexamining the validity of the present commitment to growth, full employment and productivity increase, with many people arguing that we must continue to operate within present idea-structures. They state that growth is desirable for an indefinite period into the future and that increased pollution is therefore tolerable.

Idea-structures are necessarily based on sets of assumptions. The assumption patterns on which man has based his thinking in the past have not been susceptible to formal proof. Again and again, the sets of assumptions being used have been proved incorrect as man's knowledge has grown. We are now once again going through the process of disproving current assumptions.

In addition, however, it is important that we recognize that sets of assumptions about the behavior of human beings are often self-validating. For example, if one believes that people react to positive and negative sanctions—the carrot and the whip—systems will be set up in such a way that people are *only* able to respond to the positive and negative sanctions built into the system. If, on the other hand, people are thought to rise to challenge, systems will be set up in such a way that creative decision-making is possible.

There are three necessary steps if we are to be able to discover the relevant new questions for the transition from the industrial era to the communications era. First, we must have an opportunity to discover credible information about the questions which concern us. Credibility depends on the point of view: a member of the Birch society is inherently incredible to a Black Muslim and vice-versa. Second, we must be able to discuss the credible information we have received so that we can discover its implications for our thinking and our action; only a few people can absorb basically new data without opportunities for dialogue. Finally, we must find ways to act on the basis of what we have learned so that we can discover the degree to which our ideas are relevant to the reality we actually confront.

* * *   * * *   * * *

With or without our active participation, society is moving through a transition from the industrial era into the communications era. The character of Teg herself represented for us, initially, the kind of personality which could develop from this training and experience.

Both authors were born in the twenties, a time of technological transition when an embryo twentieth-century technology, strong enough to be culturally destructive, but too weak to provide organization, was supplemented and frequently replaced by psychological control. Victories went to the psychologically and culturally strong. We therefore internalized an attitude of "facing up to things" or "grace under pressure." In the absence of other mechanisms, we laughed at problems and dangers.

Teg's personality is partly a product of fifty more years of the new technology. In her experience, technological organization has long been established; she therefore meets her problems with a technique, not a smile. She would regard us as amiable incompetents, facing situations with misplaced gallantry, when we should be applying technology to find a solution. We find Teg cold and colorless on the surface, a protagonist who is less interesting than the other personalities in the book. We are sure that some readers will share our own lack of appreciation for the skill and intelligence Teg uses to relate positively to her technological world.

We can sympathize with, if we cannot share, Teg's problem of technique outlook. We also know that her emotional and personal problems are already shared by some of today's young people. The recent movement toward a warm communality appears to be foundering in a morass of poverty and sickness and mutual exploitation due to a lack of organizing principles. The communal all-for-all is becoming the pseudo-romantic two-for-each-other and seems to be moving toward one-for-one. Crude eroticism has suppressed fantasy along with hypocrisy: now a neo-prudery is supplanting the eroticism, but the fantasy is still suppressed. In education, everyone is talking about supporting the child's imagination, or giving it free rein, and almost everyone is afraid to do it. The seeds of the Teg-type personality are present now. If society wishes for warm, sensitive, imaginative personalities in 1994, the effort must be made now. "Events" will not be to blame for the effects of tendencies which are *already* evident.

We first conceptualized Teg as an anti-hero, the occasional protagonist of the sixties: the young man moving through situations, observing, uninvolved, offering nothing, accepting little. We were searching for a central character who would both represent his world and comment on it. But we began to see that this creature of fatigued apathy, a stock-figure of science-fiction, was an unlikely choice for the technologically-based world of a quarter century into the future, whose problems would result from the situation in the early seventies and not the after-effects of World War II. We wanted our character to move through psychological space rather than the conspicuous consumption, technology-to-the-fore world of the fifties and sixties— a world reflected in the hardware orientation of so much recent science fiction.

The answer to our requirements was to make Teg a woman, one of the few female protagonists in futurist writing. Teg uses her technology merely as support system; she observes the parts of her world as functioning in relation to each other, not to herself. The physical, even the Multihogan structure, is perceived by her in terms of social and psychological organization as we ourselves perceive it.

More importantly, Teg, as a woman, is able to resolve her mental struggle between the person she was, and still is outwardly, and the person she wants to become. She is not prevented from so doing by the need for ego-protection. By the end of the book, Teg has used the communications available to her to analyze her experience and learn from it.

* * *   * * *   * * *

It is the maximal use of communications and the willingness to learn from experience which we see as the routes into the future, a better future than that outlined in *Teg's 1994*. There is no need for the detours taken by Teg's world. Once able to identify negative trends, we can already change their direction. All of the events in *Teg's 1994* are based on present tendencies or trends—some are positive (synergetic) and others negative (entropic).

In the three years since Teg was conceptualized, what has happened? Of the early seventies, trends discussed in *Teg's 1994:*

● the neo-Luddite revolt, which acts to prevent the introduction of modern technology—or to destroy it—is also growing rapidly. It is gaining support both from those who fear the loss of their jobs and also from those who hope to return to the ways of an earlier, simpler era.

● the consumers' revolt is moving beyond its initial attacks on shoddy merchandise into a general challenge against a materialistic culture.

● the Anti-Bureaucratic Coalition (ABC) has not yet been fully realized, but many elements required for its creation are being generated by the consumer and neo-Luddite revolts.

● the Planning Party, or new political party, has not yet emerged. There is, early in 1971, no evidence that a new party of this type will develop on the required scale to win the 1972 election with a fraction over a quarter of the total votes cast. However, the fragmentation of the two traditional political parties has begun and will unquestionably continue.

There are several parts to this book:

a) the foregoing introduction

b) the text of *Teg's 1994* and appendices (together comprising a computer record of the experience of Teg, a young girl who is awarded an Orwell fellowship for 1994 and travels around the world in an attempt to understand the significance of the events of the past twenty-five years and her own future role.

c) an analysis of the reactions we have received from readers during the period the book has been available. (We have left the text (b) unchanged so that you can see the reasons for these reactions.)

d) a brief analysis of various ways in which one can view the future and a summary of our own views about conceptualizing it.

e) the concept basis for the Multihogan and a reader's response.

We believe that this volume is best read in the order in which it is printed—at least for the first time. Some of you, however, may find it easier to read the analysis (d) before the text (b).

Forward!

Robert Theobald
J. M. Scott
Wickenburg, Arizona
March 1971

CHRONOLOGY OF EVENTS
1970 - 1994

1970	Anti-Bureaucratic Coalition created.
1971	Planning Party created from among the most aware members of both Democratic and Republican parties.
1972	Planning Party wins elections.
Throughout seventies	Continuing decline in the efficiency of industrial-era infrastructure.
Throughout seventies	Many colleges and universities collapse.
Throughout seventies	Decline of cities, revivification of smaller, decentralized communities.
Throughout seventies	Ecological thinking replaces economic thinking.
1975	Statement on desirability of world citizenship by 500 liberal-humanists.
1976	Planning Party wins again.
Mid-seventies	Neo-Luddite revolt leading to high levels of inefficiency in operation of technological infrastructure.
Mid-seventies	Consumer revolt against misleading advertising, planned obsolescence.
Mid-seventies	Critically high levels of tension between abundance-regions and scarcity-regions.
Late seventies	Significant attempts to create world parliament.

1979	Scientists Synergy. Those involved refuse to circulate deliberately distorted or falsified information with two major effects: a) overwhelming victory of Planning Party in 1980 followed by development of fundamentally different style of politics. b) increased cooperation and transfer of ecofacts between abundance-regions and scarcity-regions.
Early eighties	Terran Communication Center developed in Hawaii.
Early eighties	Problem / Possibility Institutes come into existence.
1984	Creation of Orwell Foundation celebrating the fact that situation in this year was not as bad as might have been expected.
Mid-eighties	Distribution of ecofacts becomes free in America, spreads to all abundance areas. Information movement replaces money movement.
Mid-eighties	INTER, OUTER and SITUATIONAL communication styles understood.
Mid-eighties	Creation of significantly new ways of structuring knowledge.
Early nineties	Growing crisis due to declining sense of responsibility in decentralized communities: decrease in pace of economic growth in scarcity regions after earlier significant increase, distortions in information flows.

TEG'S 1994
TEXT

........Transmission By Synergy Documents: A Participation Communication Service ....

The following series of documents is a Level 5 selection from the record by "Teg" of her 1994 Orwell Fellowship Year. The full text is also available. First versions of audio and video materials will be available in four weeks at Level 5.

All names have, of course, been deleted or changed. The usual exception is made for references to material produced before 1980. Sequential initials have been used for those interviewed by Teg, first names for others. Requests for further information should be sent to 111-212-000-5737.

Facilitation. This record contains insights about changes in socio-techno gestalt systems as perceived by an outside observer—"Teg."

Difficulties. The documents in this series originate from a number of sources and the communication-styles vary accordingly. With the exception of technical discussions in INTER which have been converted into Teg's SITUATIONAL, all documents have been left in their original styles. Subscribers will, therefore, encounter some difficulty with the differences between their own SITUATIONAL and Teg's SITUATIONAL, as well as between their own SITUATIONAL and that used in the communities where Teg conducts interviews.

Many of the documents are preceded by a statement by the writer which reflects his or her state of mind: this remains in the original OUTER communication-style.

1

Queries and We recommend the re-reading of this report at three-monthly in-
Comments. tervals over a year. Automatic reminders will, of course, be issued.

The following documents are contained in this report:

SECTION I: Introduction—First month at Owl Rock

DOCUMENT 1. Letter from Ben, Synergist, Teg's Recommender for Orwell Fellowship, to Teg. (January 1, 1994)

DOCUMENT 2. Record entry by Teg: First day as Orwell Fellow. (January 1, 1994)

DOCUMENT 3. Welcoming remarks by Hassan, General Facilitator of Orwell Foundation. (January 2, 1994)

DOCUMENT 4. Record entry by Teg: Second day at Owl Rock. (January 2, 1994)

DOCUMENT 5. Summary prepared by Orwell Foundation on Invisible College and P/P Institutes. (Distributed January 2, 1994)

DOCUMENT 6. Record entry by Teg: Owl Rock living and Najo Hills experimentation. (January 3, 1994)

DOCUMENT 7. Letter from Teg to father: re living technologies at Owl Rock. (January 5, 1994)

DOCUMENT 8. Record entry by Teg: Conversation with Luna. (January 6, 1994)

DOCUMENT 9. Letter from Teg to mother re Emotion-Control Pill. (January 15, 1994)

DOCUMENT 10. Tel from Teg to Hassan, General Facilitator of Orwell Foundation: re Olaf. (January 17, 1994)

DOCUMENT 11. Letter from Teg to Hassan: re decision to leave Owl Rock early. (January 22, 1994)

DOCUMENT 12. Letter from Hassan to Teg: re Teg's role in Owl Rock entropy. (January 24, 1994)

DOCUMENT 13. Record entry by Teg: re cross-cultural inter-action. (January 27, 1994)

SECTION II: LEARNING—Months two through six

DOCUMENT 14. Computer Summary Type 2 (with quotes) of interviews by Teg with Historian, A. (February 18, 1994)

DOCUMENT 15. Post-comments by Teg on interviews with A, Historian. (February 20, 1994)

DOCUMENT 17. Information Print-Out: Abundance-Region Terran Credit Card: use in scarcity regions. (prepared January 1993)

DOCUMENT 18. Main points of introductory statement by B, Scientist, with pre-comments by Teg. (March 5, 1994)

DOCUMENT 19. Record entry by Teg: re high-evening by the Great Wall. (March 28, 1994)

DOCUMENT 20. Letter from Teg to peers in Quebec: re educational system in sixties. (April 14, 1994)

DOCUMENT 21. Outline of film prepared for apprentices by C, Educational Facilitator. (created November, 1993)

DOCUMENT 22. Lecture by D, Economist/Ecologist, during third rites-de-passage of Yvonne, his granddaughter and apprentice, with pre-comments by Teg. (May 17, 1994)

Queries and Comments.

right to nominate Orwell Fellow for 1996. (December 15, 1994)

Queries and Comments.

DOCUMENT 35. Teg's Auto-Bio: Short Form. (prepared December 1994)

DOCUMENT 36. Tel from Teg to Hassan: re closing of Teg's Orwell Fellowship record. (December 23, 1994)

DOCUMENT 37. Tel from Teg to all contacts during Orwell Year. (December 23, 1994)

DOCUMENT 38. Tel from Hassan to All Participant Communication Services (December 27, 1994)

SECTION 1
INTRODUCTION -
1ST MONTH AT OWL ROCK

........**Letter from Ben, Synergist, Teg's Recommender for Orwell Fellowship, to Teg** *(Document 1)*.......................

Dear Teg,

Morning, January 1, 1994

Conditions. Computer-ideal within Quebec-home-dome: hip-high snow outside. I'll never get used to the contrast.

Personal Attitude. New Year's dayish.

Text. As I write this you're just on your way for the month-long introduction to your Orwell Fellowship, prior to a year of travel. I know that you're still surprised that I nominated you rather than Dayan or Bucky, for you always thought that our continuing disagreement meant that I did not appreciate your potential.

It's precisely because Dayan and Bucky seem to want to be not more than followers and you are already moving out of the apprentice role that we both have the possibility of benefiting from your travel. I'm not going to tell you now what my expectations for synergy are; if I did, it would certainly bias your perceptions of your experience. You should know, however, that I have already written you a letter which I intend to give you at the end of the year.

There are two things I forgot to discuss with you at our last meeting before you left. First, the Orwell Foundation is more important than you will probably realize until later. Its Fellowships have already formed a link between the succeeding generations because the ties between synergetic facilitators—like me—who recommend, and the apprentice—like you—who is recommended almost always continue and strengthen. In addition, many interviewees and interviewers discover common interests and thus new linkages between problem/possibility areas develop. The potential of the Foundation is, however, not fully apparent today because its potential has grown beyond the understanding of the liberal-humanists who founded it.

Second, you have learned to recognize that chronological age limits and facilitates different potentials at different life-periods and you are, therefore, better equipped to manage a year's continuous travel than I would have been at your age. We didn't perceive much of this in the thirties; "young people" up to age twenty-one were meant to be seen and not heard, or even get hurt! We now know that the time to understand different perceptual views is, indeed, in the third life-period between the ages of fourteen and twenty-seven, but we also know that most people's psychological stability at this time is only just equal to the strain involved.

If you were less courageous by nature and less prone to take on any challenge that arises—you're a type Leo—I wouldn't have raised new points today. But I know they won't worry you. I wish I were going with you. Make sure you key all your material through my communicator—let *me* choose what I want to read.

I envy you,
Ben

. . . . .Record entry by Teg: First day as Orwell Fellow *(Doc-*
ument 2). . . . .

Late evening, January 1, 1994

Conditions. Personally-controlled atmosphere. My communications
carrel in the Multihogan Complex. My carrel-mate not here. Nobody
down here tonight. The other carrels and the communications workroom are empty.

Personal attitude. Anticipatory! Happy to be back in a hogan in
Arizona.

Text. It was marvelous approaching the Hogan Complex early this
evening and seeing the three big Multihogans, each with a roof-high
pair of lighted New Year trees on the entrance platform. They were
grouped together in the middle of a cluster of Hogan lodges with
trees on either side of the back main entrance. For a moment the
desert disappeared and I was back this morning in Quebec on the
way to the airport, taking a last look at the stand of dense green firs
surrounding the home-dome, which glistened in the sunlight against
the bank of snow.

As the lugger started down the western slope of the hill and
turned right, I saw a girl, not more than twenty-five years old,
come out onto the entrance platform of the Northern Multihogan.
As we stopped at the platform, she said: "You must be Integra and
Mitzel. I'm Luna, your facilitator. Welcome to Owl Rock." The
other girl (who seems about fifteen years old!) looked as surprised
as I felt. I had expected all the facilitators to be in the fourth-life
period, probably around forty.

Luna led us to our personal rooms, in apartment N.E. upper; we
found a Japanese girl, Michiko, already installed in the third room.
Michiko is even smaller than I and looked lost in her huge room.
Mitzel's limited luggage is almost entirely composed of drawing

materials and equipment. I've brought extra clothes for culturally
approximating the appearance of the community residents I will
be visiting this year. I can't understand why I've been given the
center room with too much northern light and too little storage,
and Mitzel is in the more shaded room with six storage spaces
and an ante-room. (I didn't understand either why Mitzel and myself have the same facilitator, but Mitzel told me that Luna's prob-
lem/possibility area is Cross-Cultural-Community-Environment so
that does cover us both.) After we'd unpacked, Luna showed us how
to work the food preparation equipment in the pantry and the garbage processor. She then demonstrated how we could connect up
communicators in our room if we wished; there are communication
outlets in each of the rooms. The new communicators they have
here certainly don't take up much space.

After we'd looked around the rest of the apartment and out on the
covered terrace, Luna took us around the Multihogan. When we came
in this afternoon by the outside entrance to our apartment, I really
couldn't see why they were called hogans at all. I don't remember
much about our hogan lodge (I was only five when we left Arizona), but I do remember the octagonal shape and the reassuring feeling of being in a temporary state of balance whenever I sat near
the central firepit and was held in place by the light from the big
windows placed at the four compass points.

Looking at this Multihogan from the outside, it seemed much too
complex to have a simple four-compass-point-nadir-zenith orientation, even if the main door did face due east. But as soon as we went
out of our apartment, and stood on the northern inner platform looking down on the Hogan Center below, the beautiful balanced feeling
came rushing back. There were the four big windows (huge! the
western wall is all glass) and a big firepit in front of the western
wall.

As far as I could tell, the only change (apart from the Hogan Center being nine times the size) is that no rooms are built on the
northern and southern inner platforms. (They are used as circula-
tion-space and for education and community meetings.) In addition,
the living space—eight pairs of identical upper and lower apart-

ments—is built out in square wings from the southeast, southwest, northwest, and northeast walls. (I must get a computer print-out comparing a Hogan Lodge and the Multihogan to clarify this.)*

Luna told us we'd have no difficulty finding our way around the Southern and Middle Multihogans as all three are exactly the same: Communications Research Multi-Family Units. We went down the northern inner-platform stairs and across the Hogan Center to the lower-level southwest staircase which leads down to the sub-basements. There are five, one under the western outside platform and one under each of the five apartment wings. The exercise room, freshers, and storage are under the outside western platform. The southwest sub-basement area is mainly for the children, apart from the first-aid room. Although there are no children in Northern Multihogan (no animals either!), Luna took us around so we could see how the Baby Room, Toddler Room, and Kindergarten related to the one-way observation corridor and the childrens' hygiene rooms and pantry. I liked the big common-room for the seven-to-thirteen-year-olds; I wish I'd had something like it during my second life-period.

As the western slope of Owl Rock is quite steep, the sub-basement of the southwest wing is full height and there's plenty of light and outside air. Except for the Baby Room, first-aid room, and the nursery pantry, the atmosphere wasn't computer-controlled and the glass doors were still open. Chilly! Luna says it seems warm during the day, even in January.

We went along the inside corridor to the southeast wing sub-basement and Luna showed us the communications workroom (atmosphere computer-controlled) and our communications carrels. I was so pleased to be back in a personally-controlled atmosphere that I asked if we could sit and talk in my carrel. Luna brought a third seat and told me about my carrel-mate, Olaf, who is in apartment S.E. upper with two other men, Mboya and Juan. They share the carrel next to us, and Mitzel and Michiko are on the other side. Luna and the other two facilitators each have a carrel at the end. Hassan, the General Facilitator, has a carrel by the hogan entrance

*See Appendix

Queries and Comments. door and the large corner carrel is occupied by the "board member." (I still haven't found out what he does.) Luna tells me I was put in with Olaf because he may experience some difficulties with communication techniques and that's one of my skills.

We continued on around the corridor to the northeast wing and discovered that our apartment was over the main storage, clothes processing, and garbage processing area. As we still had half-an-hour left till dinner time, Luna took us along to the northwest wing, showed us the large and small dining rooms, the kitchens, the frozen food and liquid storage, and the other stords.

We continued on around the corridor to the northeast wing and discovered that our apartment was over the main storage, clothes processing, and garbage processing area. As we still had hal-an-hour left till dinner time, Luna took us along to the northwest wing, showed us the large and small dining rooms, the kitchens, the frozen food and liquid storage, and the other stores.

She then took us down into the valley so that we could see how the Owl Rock Hogan Complex looked from the west. Beautiful! A variation on how it looked from the east, on top of the hill. Small lighted trees in front of the Hogan Lodges, one huge one on the western platform of the Northern and Southern Multihogans, and in front of the Middle Multihogan, jutting out into the valley like a pleasure-ship at night; the Middlehogan swimming pool surrounded by planted trees covered with lights.

........Welcoming remarks by Hassan, General Facilitator of Orwell Foundation *(Document 3)***..............................**

11:30-11:47, January 2, 1994

Owl Rock Northern Hogan Center.

Text. Good morning everyone. And to the 1994 Orwell Fellows, welcome! We're grateful to the Owl Rock Communications Consentive and the Najo Hills Research Community for inviting us as their guests. If you turn your heads and look up at the inner platforms

you will see that most of Owl Rock's 148 consentive members are
with us this morning. After these brief remarks, there will be a celebration buffet so that the consentive members can meet the Orwell
Fellows and Facilitators.

First, I'd like to tell you about Najo Hills and Owl Rock. Then
I'll make a few points about your role as Orwell Fellows.

If you look past me out of the western window wall, you will see,
on the tops of the surrounding hills, the roofs of other Hogan Complexes, very much like Owl Rock. These hilltop Hogan Complexes,
together with those on some of the valley-floors, form the Najo
Hills Research Community. Najo Hills began in 1978 with the creation of the Sidewinder Stream Agricultural Research Consentive,
which you can see down the valley. Sidewinder was founded by a
group of agriculturalists researching minimal water-use for common
root-vegetables. It has since expanded its activities and is currently
engaged in developing new food products with minimal moisture
needs.

The total population of Najo Hills now approaches five thousand.
The Multihogan complexes vary in size according to the type of research
being done. Sidewinder is the largest, with 800 people in twenty
Multihogans and seventy Hogan Lodges. Picture Rock, with fifty
people in two Multihogans, is the smallest. I hope that during the
month you will find time to sample the variety of activities and at-
mospheres of Najo Hills' twenty consentives.

Your temporary home-consentive, Owl Rock, began five years ago
with a father-and-sons communications research team who built the
middle Multihogan. They have since been joined by the group of
communications researchers you see here this morning. Two years
ago they built the Northern and Southern Multihogans so that they
could invite outside groups here in order to observe their communication patterns.

As most of you already know, the right of general selection of site
for each year's introduction-month is given to one Fellow, chosen by
lot. This year Boris exercised his right in choosing Arizona. The
specific decision to contact Owl Rock was our choice at the Foundation, and it was made for three reasons:

Queries and
Comments.

1. The physical arrangements and equipment seemed appropriate to our purposes.

2. Living in a multi-culture, multi-activity research community would facilitate the work of our multi-interest Fellows and facilitators and be more appropriate as an environment for their several cultures.

3. This is my first year as General Facilitator of the Orwell Foundation. We felt that we could all learn much from Owl Rock's observation and analysis of Orwell's inter-cultural and interaction patterns.

The Orwell Foundation was created ten years ago in 1984, by a group of liberal-humanists. It was felt that Orwell should be honored for his role in warning of possible entropic patterns, particularly in his book, *1984*, thus helping us to perceive the need for a more humane terran society. Twelve annual Orwell Fellowships for synergetic research were created, each providing for one year of unlimited travel and research. I was a Fellow myself during the first year.

Most Fellows in previous introduction-months have found that the best way to get a sense of the synergetic potential of the year is to study print-outs of the records of previous Fellows: these always cover the fellowship year and often later developments in the Fellow's life. (I suspect you'll read mine first! I should warn you that my views have changed considerably since my Orwell year.) Don't forget that this highly unusual permission to use personal records is provided on a trust basis for Orwell-related people only—nothing can be used beyond the Foundation without specific permission.

This is not a suitable time to make you fully aware of the size of the challenge you've undertaken, but I must remind you of the new rights and responsibilities you have just acquired. Even though you will normally remain apprentices until the end of your third life-period, your Orwell Fellowship relates you to the Invisible College and provides you with a high priority suffix to your identity number—you will keep this suffix unless you cease to be interested in the Invisible College, or unless you lose the right to the suffix through

deliberate and continued misuse. (We have had no such case in the
history of the Orwell Fellowships.) In another sense, you have
already moved out of the apprenticeship because, as 1994 Fellows,
it is your right to choose the person who will in turn nominate a
1996 Fellow.

Your major immediate responsibilities include fuller use of communications than many of you have been used to. I'll be available in
the communications workroom throughout the afternoon, as will
members of the Owl Rock Communication Consentive, for any immediate explanations. (The Owl Rock people and myself will, of course,
continue to be available throughout this month.) In particular, some
of you will have to learn the telins techniques which make it possible for you to be always available. This may be initially trouble-
some for those who have not previously participated in a fully developed communications net.

Because your new responsibilities started yesterday, I wish to recommend that you read the summary document we've prepared on
the Invisible College as soon as you can.

And now we'll go into the western platform for the celebration buffet. The chef has prepared one of the high-dishes from each of your
home-communities and marked it with the name of the Fellow from
that community. If you would like information on how the dish is
customarily eaten, I suggest that you talk to the appropriate Fellow.

........**Record entry by Teg: Second day at Owl Rock** (Document 4)...

After lunch, January 2, 1994

Conditions. Personally-controlled atmosphere.
Our communications carrel. Olaf trying out communications techniques.

Personal Attitude. Full of eleven high-dishes! I thought I should try
them all. And confused! Probably some connection. I eat a minimal
lunch usually, and often alone. I'm pleased that Mitzy and Michiko
will snack-lunch in our pantry too.

Text. As Juan said, *que muchadumbre!*—what a mob! If it hadn't
been for meeting the Northern Hogan residents at dinner last night,
everybody at lunch would have been a blur—except, of course, Michiko and Mitzy and Olaf and Luna and our very impressive General
Facilitator, Hassan.

There were just the twelve of us at dinner last night, but it seemed
a large crowd. Probably when I know them all it won't seem such
a lot. As we had no guests, we used the large round table and we
were all assigned our seats—apparently according to some idea of
"social mixing"! We were seated male-female-male-female all
around the table. On my right, I had Mboya, on my left, Juan.
They're Olaf's roommates and seem to be getting on splendidly together; they both have big ha-ha laughs and are working on animal ecology. I felt like a deer between a couple of buffalo! Not
that they were paying much attention to me; they were far too occupied with their other neighbors. Juan was charming Luna, and
Mboya was really drawing Michiko out. I was surprised she could
be so talkative and laugh so much.

Olaf sat between Michiko and Mitzy; in spite of Michiko's little efforts and Mitzy's on-and-off attempts, he hardly entered the conversation at all. Mitzy was chattering mostly to the "Board Member,"
who seems to be a nice, friendly man, and who was being very
attentive to Hassan's wife on his right. Hassan sat next to his wife
with the other two facilitators beyond him. If they *had* to allocate
places, I couldn't see why they didn't put Olaf next to his facilitator,
who could have talked to him about work, instead of grouping all
of us Fellows on one side of the table to "socialize." Mboya and
Juan are fun, even if a bit overpowering. Juan's standard greeting
is *Arriba*! (Forward!) Typical of his type to want to get on with
things.

Lunch today was interesting too. I didn't really mind the crush once
I'd begun to sort out the six Fellows in Southern Hogan from their
spouses and facilitators and the Middle Hogan consentive group.

Boris, the Russian, whose choice was Arizona, is not at all bear-like! Tall, thin, dreamy, and doesn't even appear overly interested in Amerinds. He's sharing the Southern Hogan S.E. upper apartment with Julius, who's Malayan and thought it was too cool to eat outside. Berthe and Marie share the S.E. lower apartment, and there are two married students and their spouses, Cha-Li-Mah and Lawrence, Carla and Carlos. Carla told me that they have *three* little C's under five years old! Carlos looks much older than the other Fellows. Juan told me after lunch that he's 27 years old. He was lucky his facilitator had the right to nominate in 1993, for otherwise it would have been too late.

On the other hand, I'm wondering if Mitzy wasn't nominated before she could benefit. She looks fifteen, is sixteen, and sometimes acts thirteen. I have the uncomfortable feeling I'm living with someone who's not out of the second life-period yet. She spends very little time in her communications carrel, a lot talking to the other Fellows and the rest outside in her corner of our covered terrace doing sketches! She says there's more light out there, but I think she really enjoys the outside environment. I thought I would too, but I don't seem to stay on the terrace, even though I have to walk along it to enter my room from the outside staircase. I haven't seen Michiko at all since last night. I'd like to talk to her because I think it will be most useful to understand something of the cultures represented by the Fellows here and their families. We have a good selection of communities: Japanese, German, Scandanavian, East African, Spanish, Russian, Malayan, Flemish, French, English, Australian, Chinese, and Latin American—besides myself! Of course, since the process of societal decentralization is now so complete, ethnic, national, or aereal origin is not a good guide to personality. I find I keep on forgetting this, however.

Distributed: January 2, 1994

Text

Definition of Invisible College

The term "Invisible College" came into being following the Scientists' Synergy of 1979 to describe those who were interested in and competent to work conceptually. The general assumption is that while conceptual skills are still rare they should receive no more recognition than practical skills. The agriculturist is as necessary to the community as the agricultural researcher, the mother facilitating in the kindergarten contributes as much to community-building as the community facilitator.

> *Note.* Many in the Invisible College are now expressing doubt about the relevancy of the conceptual/practical dichotomy. Given the recent changes in patterns of learning, it would seem that the conceptual skills of those in the first three life-periods have now increased to the point where "conceptual" or "practical" is simply a choice of work-techniques.

Entry into Invisible College

Conceptual skills are usually clearly perceptible by the age of fourteen—the beginning of the third life-period. Those who wish to be related to the Invisible College usually enter into an apprenticeship with a synergetic facilitator whose problem/possibility area (p/p area) is congruent with their initial interests. Some apprentices remain with a single facilitator; others find it helpful to learn with several, nearly always consecutively.

As soon as an apprentice has learned the basic skills (this usually does not take more than a year), he works on a part or parts of a project. He is fundamentally responsible for his parts of the project—only referring back to his facilitator when he perceives that a decision would significantly affect the long-run direction of the project. Later, the facilitator obtains projects for his apprentices which are suited to their talents, interests, and level of competence. Finally, the apprentice moves out on his own and is considered part of the Invisible College.

> *Note.* Certain industrial-era patterns still exist which complicate relationships between facilitators and apprentices. There are a significant number of young people who still want to be followers—parroting the knowledge and style of their facilitator, rather than apprentices who wish to become independent of their facilitator. There are also still a surprising number of "facilitators" who do not understand synergy and make their apprentices learn what they already know rather than encouraging them to move out on their own.

Contacting Invisible College Facilitators

Usually an individual, consentive, or community which needs help on a project in a specific p/p area will know a facilitator who is interested in the p/p area. They will ask him or her to take on the project or else to recommend another facilitator.

Other individuals, consentives, and communities will not have easy access to facilitators. To meet their needs, data on facilitators is available from computer records. Information can be requested about those facilitators available to work on projects in a given p/p area. The communicator print-out in response to a request of this type will contain a list of names and tel numbers as well as information about degree of availability and competence. Information about availability is recorded by the facilitator himself; those requesting it can thus ascertain whether the facilitator is likely to be available. Information about competence is based on the assessment of those with whom the facilitator has worked over the past two years. (The initial competence assessment of apprentices as they move out to work on their own is provided by their former facilitators.) Once a preliminary choice of facilitators has been made, a computer print-out listing past work can be obtained. This is compiled by the facilitator himself.

Queries and Comments.

Queries and Comments.

Interaction within Institutes of the Invisible College

In the fifteen years since the scientists synergy, the Invisible College movement has become worldwide. Those working in each p/p area are considered to be interacting members of the p/p area Institute; some facilitators choose to belong to two or even three Institutes.

Each Institute has a Communication Center; these are geographically scattered throughout the world. Those responsible for the continuing functioning of each Institute are especially promising apprentices concerned with the p/p area. They initially worked with an individual facilitator and have chosen to move to the Communition Center of the Institute for a period of years. The Communications Center is responsible for compiling and diffusing information about developments in the p/p area, using dialogue-focusers, dialogue-discussions, and psychebanks.

Working with these apprentices are interaction facilitators chosen from the total membership of the Institute. These attend regular annual meetings and also spend a few months at the Center during their period of responsibility (three to seven years) in order to facilitate the work of the apprentices. The interaction facilitators are also responsible for perceiving possible crises before they arise and calling emergency meetings to determine methods of avoiding them.

Each person who is assessed at the ninth level of competence or above in a p/p area can expect to be called to serve in his Institution once in his fourth life-period. It is generally agreed that the call should be accepted; at most, it can be postponed for a limited time because of a critical research project.

In order to avoid any possibility of the Center's work becoming entropic, provision is made for any member of the Institute, or any person from the general public to participate in meetings of interest to them.

The Terran Center

The Terran Center in Hawaii is composed of two Interaction Centers which work with p/p Institutes:

The Terran Communications Center (TCC). This is organized according to the same principles as the specific Communication Centers, but its scope is far wider; it attempts to comprehend the overall terran pattern of development. It contains the largest number of interaction facilitators (91) chosen from among all p/p areas. Those who are selected for the TCC must necessarily have not only a comprehensive view, but also high levels of communication skills. Calls to this Center are accepted immediately, however inconvenient they may be. Specific p/p Institute Communication Centers are responsible for informing the TCC about developments which seem likely to have general significance, and they are entitled to call upon the TCC if an issue cuts across several areas.

2. *Terran Synergy Game Center.* This is designed to simulate developments in any p/p area. Simulation principles have now been understood to the point where any specific problem, however complex, can be examined with the aid of this technique. The goal is to discover the points at which existing synergies (movement toward higher levels of organization) need to evolve in the new directions and existing entropies (movement toward lower levels of organization) should be reversed.

Communication techniques within the Invisible College

Every member of the Invisible College is expected to be available for communication at all times. The portable telins equipment weighing eight ounces is used for audio purposes and is carried at all times. It contains provisions for three readiness states:

Queries and Comments.

a) Willing to receive all communications.
b) Busy.
   Only essential communications should be made by telins. Other messages should be routed as communicator print-outs.
c) Do not disturb.
   Only messages of extreme urgency should be communicated by telins. All other messages should be routed as communicator print-outs.

........**Record entry by Teg: Owl Rock Living and Najo Hills experimentation** *(Document 6)*.............................

After dinner, January 3, 1994

Conditions. My room, using communicator. Alone.

Personal Attitude. Exasperated.

Text. I'm finding it very difficult to accept the contrast between all this environmental encouragement toward socializing at dinner and the lack of any possibility of interacting with my roommates in the apartment. There is no social room for us to meet in and we each take our breakfast and lunch snacks at different times. The living arrangements were conceived badly.

Carla and Carlos, in Southern Hogan, have a different living difficulty. I visited them after lunch and they are squeezed into one apartment with their three little C's. The six-month-old baby is sleeping in their room and they're not getting much sleep and they were already tired from their travel. The Middle Hogan nursery has suggested to Carla that she bring all three children over during the day, but she doesn't want to because she feels that the family should be together in this strange environment. Poor Carlos, it must be difficult enough being older, without missing sleep and facing family crises.

Olaf is also totally miserable in his apartment. Mboya and Juan have taken to fetching large quantities of frozen food and eating long lunches while sitting out on the terrace. They also hold noisy discussions—he feels out of it, but hesitates to join in. In spite of my best efforts, he's not yet comfortable with the telins either.

Last night when we had the Southern Hogan people over for dinner (that made 24 of us and the tables were put together to make a huge oval!) Olaf was seated between Berthe and Marie and seemed even *more* miserable than the first night. Perhaps it wasn't only him—the general atmosphere wasn't very happy anyway. Once again, the third-life period people were on one side of the table, the fourth life-period on the other. (As Luna *is* twenty-five, she must have felt straddled between the two groups.) I was flanked by Boris and Julius and couldn't seem to get them to talk about their home communities at all.

After dinner I walked over with the chef and his wife to see their Hogan Lodge, as I wanted to see how much it resembled what I would remember of my first home. It appeared that the chef was *also* irritated about dinner. He has moved to Owl Rock for two years from his home Food Preparation and Presentation Consentive in order to work on sedentary diets. He has already planned to give us his new stuffed plums dessert before Sidewinder sent up a new squash along with the other vegetables and requested that he try it out this evening. Most people liked the squash—tomato-colored with an oniony taste—but although I thought the color appetizing, I hate onions so I didn't like it. I enjoyed the stuffed plums though and told the chef. He was pleased and said I should visit his consentive for an all-experimental meal. I said I'd like to as I was interested in the variety of experimentation here. That's really true, but I'm not sure that I'd like living in a reciprocally-experimental community like Najo Hills.

The chef's Hogan Lodge seemed very like my family's as I remember it; the only difference was in the equipment. Their son, age twelve, was in his room working at his communicator on *very* high levels of music print-outs. The chef said that he would be celebrating his second rites-de-passage just after we've left in February. (As early as Mitzy!)

His little girl, age six, was with some friends in her room, sitting around the four-by-six foot screen watching Film Classics designed for Gestalt-Imagination-Stimulation. The whole scene looked like photogarphs of children watching the old television sets in the sixties! A Level 3 classic, *Fantasia,* was just finishing. We stayed for the beginning of the Level 4 *Wizard of Oz.* The beginning is still one of my favorites. It reminded me of watching with my brother at home, but these children have much better equipment than we had.

........**Letter from Teg to father: re living technologies at Owl Rock** *(Document 7)*...

Dear Parent,

Midday, January 5, 1994

Conditions. We're having a totally unusual heatwave. Everybody is in the pool except Julius, who says we're not acting sensibly. As he's just left the Malayan sun, his view is reasonable enough.

Personal attitude. Everything looks good to me today.

Text. There's some new gadgetry here which will prevent my obligation of presenting a complete record of my Fellowship year from taking up time I could use in other ways. I've chosen a four milli-meter movie camera which works without any extra lighting; I place it in one corner of the room and it reacts to mobile heat sources. It automatically takes in all of the room if people are moving; if everybody is still and one person is talking, it concentrates on the speaker. The film needs no development and is reusable. I get an automatic audiotape in addition. (Some people are considering taking around the equipment for making all-sense tapes. I consider its thirty-pound weight unjustifiable. My luggage is already too heavy.)

To get a complete transcript of an interview, etc., I enter the audiotape into the communicator, set it for language, and wait for the print-out. The computer will run through the tape as many times as necessary to screen out the accent, then I get the print-out. These newer systems of computer translation have finally eliminated the old slowness and inaccuracy, but the difficulties with communication styles remain. Obviously, nobody expects to be able to understand technical interactions in INTER style if the topic discussed is outside his field. But people still feel that they should be able to fully understand conversations in another community's SITUATIONAL, and even expect to understand everything expressed by somebody thinking aloud in OUTER—as though, somehow, the machine could add social and psychological insights while doing the translation.

Two other things. First, you'd be interested in some of the living technology here. The community is fully self-sufficient in power —sun, heat-pumps, etc. They haven't had to use their emergency main power cable connection in their five years of existence. Water, of course, is the usual problem in Arizona and there's maximum prevention of loss by evaporation. Najo Hills is big enough to have its own sewage-breakdown unit with fertilizer and water as the prime resulting products. Sidewinder, the agricultural consentive, uses the water and fertilizer. I'm glad, for I still don't like knowing I'm drinking treated sewage.

Second, I've learned from the Owl Rock Communications Consentive

Queries and Comments. that there's concern about the capacity of the present communications infrastructue to handle peak loads. Analysis suggests human, rather than machine, failure. Can you let me know if there are other technological systems which are not operating at theoretical capacity?

Forward,

Teg

........Record entry by Teg: Conversation with Luna *(Document 8)*..

After lunch, January 6, 1994

Conditions. Alone in my room at communicator.

Personal attitude. Full! Again! I must stop eating those big lunches, but I certainly didn't want to refuse when Luna invited me to her apartment to discuss my Auto-Bio over lunch.

Text. Luna teled me at 11:30 and we arranged to meet on the western platform so that we could go for a walk before collecting the food for lunch. As one of my interests is biology / ecology, we went down the hill to the slope above Sidewinder to look at the Desert Ecology Appreciation Area. The Sidewinder people got the idea after noticing that morning and evenings the area around the small upper drainage pool attracted the small animals, and the small animals attracted the larger desert fauna whose prey they are.

At midday in January there's nothing there but grey-brown vegetation waiting for its annual life in March and April, but the semi-circular clear screen which curved round the water-filled depression was printed with information and pictures of the flowers and plants in full bloom. There was also information and pictures on the fauna, with everything life-size and startlingly realistic, including the snakes. It was disappointing that there were no live animals for comparison with the pictures, and Luna suggested we return one evening.

As we were coming back up the slope, Luna said that I should look closely at the Middle Hogan terraces. I saw that although the sets of windows of the apartments were different shapes and sizes, it wasn't very noticeable because they were masked by the symmetrical arches of the covered terraces. Luna explained that this diversity-in-uniformity is an old Mediterranean building pattern; it seems to be connected with the need for shade and air-circulation, so that all the buildings in any community are oriented according to the same directional principle. That's probably why the Navajo and Mediterranean building patterns can be used together.

On our way home we passed the Owl Rock swimming pool just below Middle Hogan and it was full of seven-to-thirteen-year-olds from the Hogan Lodges and Middle Hogan taking part of their daily exercise before going to the dining room in the food-preparation wing for midday lunch. Luna wanted to see how the one-to-six-year-olds liked the tomato-onion squash which was going to be served to them today, so we went round the southeast corner, by the nursery wading pool and exercise area, and into the Observation Corridor of the childrens' wing. We passed by the Baby Room: they were satiated and peacefully asleep in their computer-controlled environment. The littlest C was there! Luna told me that Carla had changed her mind about bringing her three little C's over to the Middle Hogan Nursery as soon as she realized that it was a team of mothers who worked in the nursery (so that the family would be together after all), and that she could choose how often she'd be part of the team. She'll be there every third day and she's already begun to work with Carlos in her non-team time.

We went along the observation corridor to the ten-months to two-year room; they were eating the tomato-onion squash pureed and obviously liking it. Luna said she thought it was mainly the color. In the next room, the three-to-six-year-olds were eating it braised with their meat, the same way it was cooked for us on our second night here. They liked it too. Evidently, nobody else dislikes onions round here!

The seven-to-thirteen-year room was empty, as they were all in the pool, but we looked in at the row of communicators (the Toddler Room had only two and the Kindergarten, four). There was an interesting display of modelled figures on shelves along one wall, which Luna said were the product of the childrens' most recently acquired skill.

As we left Middle Hogan, we met one of the mothers taking the toddlers' colorful play material for recycling. She explained to us that the traditional sand-box could not be used here in the desert, because of the problem of snakes, so the man-made materials laboratory in the Basic Materials Consentive had evolved this play-material. It consists of small dodecahedral structures, covered in "hairs" which stick to each other so that they can be used to create forms; it's also soft and pleasurable to handle. The play-material is recyclable exactly like my dresses: you put the material in for breakdown and cleaning, then you dial for color, pattern, form, and size.

Luna collected the frozen food and salad from the food storage corridor in Northern Hogan, and then we went to her N.W. upper apartment. She is alone and says its too big for her way of living. After she had put the food in to prepare, we sat down to talk about my short Auto-Bio. Luna got a print-out from her communicator and read it aloud:

Prepared: October 1993.

Born: Arizona, 1973, August 3

Rites-de-Passage: 1st life-period to second: Quebec

Rites-de-Passage: 2nd life-period to third: Quebec

Major strengths. Good cross-cultural communication skills.

Languages. Excellent English
Excellent French.
Good Chinese.
Good Spanish.
Some Portuguese.

Communication Styles. Practice in OUTER, particularly OUTER-INTER conversations. SITUATIONAL primarily based on Quebec patterns.

Other Community Experiences. Stratford, England: a small theatre-oriented community. Limoges, France: oriented to ceramic arts.

Life events. Until age five I was in Arizona. My father took part in the Scientists Synergy of 1979, and this forced my family to move out of Arizona. My parents chose to move to Quebec. This move was difficult for both my parents. As a result I am inclined to be over-emotional.

Acculturation during my second life-period took place primarily among people interested in the Invisible College. However, Quebec is a balanced community and I obtained a wide range of learning experiences. In particular, my peer group took advantage of the many local environments and became knowledgeable in biology / ecology.

My second rites-de-passage were around my decision to be apprenticed to Ben, a synergist, living in Quebec. During the last six years I have been working with Ben, who researches the intercommunity dynamics which have emerged following the decentralization movement of the seventies and eighties. He recognizes that this development has so far been synergetic, but he has begun to perceive changes in direction and has anticipated the possibility of entropy.

Ben has recommended me for an Orwell Fellowship in 1994. I argued with him about this choice, suggesting

that there were other people in our Quebec community who
would benefit more from the opportunity. Having failed to convince him, I accepted the Fellowship and intend to spend
the year discovering what I can most usefully do during the
second half of my third life-period.

Luna was particularly interested in the fact that my family experienced a traumatic move when I was five and said she'd noticed
that I seemed to be living at a dysfunctionally high emotional level.
I told her it wouldn't be so high if the living and social arrangements
here functioned a little better! In particular I find it irritating that:

1. We seem to have no choice about interacting socially
in the common rooms—it's not that I'm unsociable but I feel
that my actions are being *engineered.* I'd like to interact
with some people, not *everyone,* and I find it difficult to
talk on this enforced equality basis with people much older
than myself, like Carlos, or much younger, like Mitzy.

2. In our apartment we have the opposite problem. There's
nowhere to interact as there's no social room and the pantry
is not designed for interaction.

3. There's a general lack of space in the Fellows' three-
room apartments. For example, Carlos and Carla and the
three little C's over in Southern Hogan are all squashed into the apartment so that the baby has to sleep in their room.
Olaf is also miserable in his room because one side gives
onto the pantry terrace and Mboya and Juan make a lot of
noise eating and talking out there. I told Luna that the *general* problem is lack of flexibility in the physical and social
arrangements.

Luna agreed that the social arrangements had been rather inflexible, but said that this was partly through misuse of the physical
arrangements which weren't really inflexible at all. We got a print-

out of apartment distribution in the two Orwell Hogans and the Middle Consentive Hogan for comparison.*

Luna said that although all the apartments had exactly the same plan and number of rooms, the Middle Hogan residents had taken far more advantage of the available flexibility. She pointed out that in Middle Hogan, just like in ours, there are two apartments shared by three adults and that their living arrangements were better because they'd made one room into a social room. She also said that she thought this improved circulation patterns so we got a three-resident comparative print-out of my apartment and the one of the apartments in the Middle Hogan.*

As we were comparing the two living-and-circulation patterns, I said that although I could see that some of my interaction difficulties obviously did result from our circulation pattern—for we seldom met—the bigger difficulty was our lack of a social room.

Luna pointed out that like the three people in Middle Hogan N.E. lower, we could use our Central Hall to sit and talk, or even better, go out on our common terrace. I reminded her about Olaf's difficulty with noise from his roommates talking outside the pantry, and she said that Olaf's facilitator had already suggested that he change rooms with Juan, moving from A, by the pantry, to C, all the way way around the terrace in the quiet corner.

Luna added that there did seem to be some constraintes about Orwell behavior patterns which surprised her after what she'd heard about Hassan. She didn't understand why the usual practice of letting people change their rooms whenever they wished hadn't been followed, why certain apartments were being left empty, and why evening meal seating was so formal. She said she was going to look into it.

*See Appendix

Queries and Comments.

Meanwhile she said that I'd get a better idea of the potential of the Multihogans if I visited the Living Design Consentive on the hill due west of Owl Rock. It was the second consentive created in Najo Hills, after Sidewinder, and it had used as model the Hogan Lodges first built in 1972. They designed the Multihogan in 1980 for multi-use and flexible living, as well as for ease and speed of construction. She pointed out, for example, that putting all the hygiene rooms together, instead of each one attached to a room, minimized maintenance which is one of the chief concerns of all communities today. The Living Design Consentive members think that the Multihogan design needs considerable rethinking because of the new technologies: they're searching for a design which will be equally flexible, but more convenient.

The design must have maximum flexibility because the apartments and sub-basements and the Hogan Center function differently from family to family and Hogan to Hogan. Sidewinder has one Multihogan occupied by a single family: twenty-four people, three generations. At Picture Rock one of the artists has a very large family (two adults and five children) in one apartment. I asked Luna how many ways there were of using the rooms, with the number of people ranging from one to seven. She didn't know, so we questioned the communicator.

Over lunch we talked about the Owl Rock Consentive members. Luna felt that other Orwell Fellows weren't making as much use of their help with communication techniques as they might. Nor with domestic arrangements, although Carla is getting on much better now. Apparently she talked with a mother from Middle Hogan who has three small children, almost the same ages as Carla's. She suggested that Carla do what everyone else does and put the baby in the ante-room instead of their room to sleep, so that he wouldn't be disturbed and fretful at night. He's sleeping much better now, and so are Carlos and Carla. They feel less crowded too.

Luna said that the Middle Hogan members considered that the apartments are adequate for two adults and two children, but that there is always crowding when there are two small children *and* a baby. As soon as children have celebrated their first rites-de-passage, they are considered mature enough to occupy the apartment under their parents, with a connecting staircase installed between the two "A" rooms. The upper one becomes the adults' (and family) social room and the lower the childrens' social room. As there is hardly ever an empty apartment underneath a growing family, this means that there has to be a general move-round in the Hogan so that the two-apartment arrangement can be organized when the eldest child reaches his second life-period. The telins is used, of course, for inter-apartment communication.

As the Najo Hills children didn't seem to be the same age as we were when we celebrated our first and second rites-de-passage, I asked Luna if the life-periods were the same: birth to six years, first life-period; seven to thirteen years, second life-period; fourteen to twenty-seven years, third life-period; and age twenty-eight beginning the fourth-life period. She said yes, exactly, but, of course, there are one or two exceptions. For example, the chef's son, who has very advanced musical knowledge and skills, is sufficiently emotionally mature that he will enter his third life-period at age twelve. Luna said that if he continues his balanced development, he will probably celebrate his third rites-de-passage at twenty-four, as she did herself.

I then asked Luna if she knew of any community which had sufficient experience with the fourth life-period to know if there needed to be additional rites-de-passage (whether there should be only one life-period after one's apprenticeship ended or many). Luna said she thought that nobody had found the answer to this yet. I asked if she thought that living in a multi-experimental community had an effect in advancing maturity. Luna said that perhaps it did in the second period, but not in the first, which was passed in more or less the same manner wherever the concept of life-periods is being used: mainly in a restricted environment, protected from overstimulation by older children and adults.

After affection-and-recognition interaction with their mothers and fathers, the babies are brought out into the Toddler Room for the beginning of socialization as soon as they can sit up. Then they pass through the usual stages of the learning process at their own speeds. As they move from early group-training and sense stimulation to the first steps in auto-training, they go from the Toddler

Room to the Kindergarten, where the adults begin to act as education facilitators. Most training in basic skills is completed in Kindergarten with intensive use of the communicators.

At age seven, after celebrating their first rites-de-passage, they move over to the Common Room for seven-to-thirteen-year-olds and work with the communicators there as well as their personal ones in their rooms. They also begin to go out every day to other Najo Hills research consentives so that they can complete their training and education and begin to have some idea of the p/p area they would like to work in. Last week the Middle Hogan seven-to-thirteens were working in the inner platform sculpture studio at Picture Rock; the figure-models we saw before lunch were their week's work.

It is perhaps during this time that they speed up their process of maturation, as compared with other children in the second life-period. They experience many activities, many skills, many family types, living patterns, and subcultures as they go around Najo Hills. Their group interchanges during INTER-OUTER discussions are very rich. It may be because they are aware of a wide range of p/p areas that they settle on their area of apprenticeship early.

I said to Luna that the childrens' multi-cultural experience must also help them when travelling in other communities and asked her if she thought my preparations for the year's travel were appropriate. We discussed my clothes and I said that I'd brought the usual recyclable wear plus some instant-clean clothes for communities where recycling equipment was not available. I brought no activities clothes because I can get them from the stores in the various communities, but my luggage is extensive anyway because I brought a large number of high-dresses. Some of these we wear at home, but most are for culturally-approximating the high-dresses of the communities I shall be visiting.

Luna said that she wasn't at all sure that I'd need them. In her experience, people are interested in seeing the high-dresses from your own community and, also, if your interaction with them is really synergetic, they will offer you a choice of their own high-dresses for a celebration. I'm not sure Luna's right; after all, everyone's experience is different. So I'll keep my luggage as it is and reorganize later in the year if necessary.

........**Letter from Teg to mother re Emotion-Control Pill** *(Document 9)*..

Dear Parent,

Afternoon, January 15, 1994 (Transmitted by telins.)

Conditions. I used one of the new quiet-copters, flew into the Grand Canyon and landed in one of the very few areas where powered vehicles are permitted. I took a mule and from where I now am the Canyon looks just as it did millenia ago. I suppose because of my racial mix, I need these conditions for making major decisions.

Personal attitude.   Post-major decision.

Text. Computer-medical-record-compilation today. No surprises. The inoculations were effective. I'm still surprised that the promotive medicine program leaves us vulnerable to so many diseases, but I suppose this was inevitable after the chemical inundation of the fifties and sixties. (I managed to beat my record for linking up to the computer: not really a fair test, for the new sensing devices here are much easier to handle.)

The computer stored my year's schedule and the communicator reminded me about the possibilities of fatigue and depression. I don't understand, for once I've assimilated the introductory research at Owl Rock most of the year's hard work is done.

Now to my decision. I'm going to use Pill 2 starting at the time of my first interview. I know you're not in favor of emotion-control although your letter transmitted this morning leaves the decision to me. (An extraordinary number of parents are still attempting persuasive-structural-parental-authority—in fact none of the deer-peers are as lucky as me.)

Don't misunderstand my decision, I'm also still against emotion-control in principle. I've met two or three twenty-year-olds who benefitted fully from the knowledge available on balancing emotional and intellectual development and whose life was not profoundly disrupted by the violence which existed in the first years of their lives. They don't need Pill 2.

But if I'm to carry through this year successfully I must clearly understand my strengths and weaknesses. I'm not trying to attribute total character development to single events, but I think we all agree that father's need to move our home during the 1979 Scientists Synergy, when I was five, did have a profound effect. Anyway, everybody who knows me, including you, agree that I tend to act without perceiving. I also tend to pick up too many emotional clues and to forget conceptual realities.

If it weren't for this year of travel, I would have waited to begin Pill 2 until I was well into the latter part of the third life-period—the time usually recommended for extended use.

There has been much interaction among the Fellows here on the choice of using, or not using, Pill 2. Three of the men will and four of the girls: two men and two girls won't and one man is undecided. I think that everybody who has decided is right. Olaf, who won't use the Pill clearly needs to recover his emotionality; he'll probably have much more difficulty doing this than I shall in lowering my emotional level.

In order to get further confirmation, I've been to the Health Consentive: they've been developing new self-tests for emotionality. They wanted me to stay around for I provided results they hadn't seen before! Anyway it was very helpful of them to reinforce my decision to start taking Pill 2 when I start interviewing on February 1.

Forward,

Teg

........**Tel from Teg to Hassan, General Facilitator of Orwell Foundations re Olaf** *(Document 10)*............................

23:11, January 17, 1994

Text. Since a meeting of Olaf with his personal facilitator two days ago, he has been suffering from acute culture shock. It's ridiculous that I should have to bring it to your attention.

Olaf has been working with the telins. He's managed with some difficulty to understand its functioning in the tel system. He and I have successfully practiced the readiness states: "Busy," and "Do not disturb." However, he doesn't see the point of practicing readiness state "Willing to receive all communications" for a certain amount of time each day in order to facilitate interaction with the other Fellows here. Neither does he understand the necessity for having the telins with him at all times.

I believe that his reluctance to interact with others is a manifestation of his underemotional state. It seems to me that this is attributable to his long period of apprenticeship with his scholar-recluse-facilitator. This facilitator considers that the tel system should be used almost exclusively for interaction with his p/p Institute.

When Olaf used OUTER to try to explain his difficulties to his Orwell Facilitator, she became angry: "You decided to accept your facilitator's recommendation for a Fellowship. May I remind you that this decision implies new responsibilities as well as rights. Can't you see that all those related to the Invisible College must be in touch at all times. We are privileged people and we must fulfill our roles." (This is a direct quote from his audiotape.)

Olaf left this interview confused; he's since been increasingly depressed and has walked around looking vacant for two days. This evening after dinner we talked in his personal room and it took me three hours—and a considerable quantity of Aquavit—to get him to tell me the story. This experience has had an entropic effect: he had already decided that the p/p area in which he has hoped to work during his fellowship year was far too narrowly drawn because his education has so far been very restricted.

Queries and Comments. I felt that sending you a tel would be the quickest way to get something done. I'd have talked to Olaf's Orwell facilitator, but I think that I might do more harm than good. Either she's in a general over-emotional state or she misunderstands both her role as facilitator and the meaning of the Invisible College.

........**Letter from Teg to Hassan re decision to leave Owl Rock early** *(Document 11)*..

After midnight, January 22, 1994

Conditions. My personal room in Quebec. A blizzard is just over and the sky is totally clear: through the heated sections of the dome, even my personal telescope makes it look as though one can touch Moon-Station 3.

Personal Attitude. Still fuming, but under control.

Text. As I told you this morning before I left, I've come home for the remaining nine days before I go to the Harlem community on the east coast of North America for my first interview. I know that you and Luna could have facilitated more learning but the arrangements at Owl Rock were increasingly entropic, at least for me. I felt desperately constrained.

The social and living arrangements at Owl Rock made our task of information assimilation and research unnecessarily difficult. I do not understand how everything we have learned about the function and functioning of community could have been so completely ignored.

The Fellows shared nothing except the fact that we had been awarded Orwell Fellowships. Our p/p areas were too far apart for us to be able to talk INTER with each other and, with rare exceptions, we failed to develop an Owl Rock SITUATIONAL. We certainly were unable to create the psychic unity necessary for interacting in OUTER.

Given the fact that none of the communication styles functioned, everyone became profoundly uncomfortable. I was no longer able to synergize.

Queries and Comments.

Backward,

Teg.

........Letter from Hassan to Teg re Teg's role in Owl Rock entropy *(Document 12)*.......................................

Dear Teg,

Late evening, January 24, 1994

Conditions. Unusual degree of dislocation created in large part by your abrupt departure. Mitzy has also left. I doubt whether she'll complete her Fellowship year. Two other Fellows are clamoring to leave. Olaf has been so discouraged by your departure that he's thinking of giving up his Fellowship. You created a dependency relationship which was not your fault but that of his Orwell Facilitator who did have unperceived emotional difficulties.

Personal attitude. Tired, impatient.

Text. I'd like to blame you for the trouble you've caused but it wouldn't be accurate to do so. I can only say that if you'd given me just a *little* time for interaction before leaving we might have been able to minimize your dissatisfaction and its entropic effects on this year's Fellowship holders.

Looking backward, I can now see, however, that somebody would inevitably act in this way this year. When I became General Facilitator eight months ago, I told the Board of Directors that I wanted to reorganize social, living, and learning patterns for the introduction-month. They agreed but asked me to wait till next year. I decided to do so and your leaving was the result.

I had originally intended to tell this year's Fellows about the anticipated changes in the introduction-month. But in the interim between my planning of the month and January 1, there was an Orwell Board Meeting where it was decided to send a Board Member to Owl Rock in order to aid me in the complete reorganization of the Orwell Fellowships. Unfortunately, while his aim was to help with the reorganization, his attitude—essentially paternalistic—toward the Fellows was still that which had prevailed since the Foundation was started.

At that time it was felt that as the Orwell Year is basically one of system-break for the Fellows they should be relieved of all unnecessary decision-making. This was the beginning of patterns which have now become entropic. So many decisions were made for the Fellows during the introduction-months of past years that desirable growth-choices were eliminated along with habit-choices which do waste time.

Even before any of the Fellows arrived at Owl Rock, the Board Member had already decided on patterns for allocation of living space, eating arrangements, etc. I had a choice between prejudicing my continued work with him on the Foundation reorganization or making *this* year's introduction-month less synergetic.

Had you come to me three days ago, we could have interacted on this entropic situation and its bad personal effects. I could have made several suggestions for mitigating it through spatial rearrangement. However, even if *all* the entropy in the introduction-month situation had been removed, there would *still* have remained your own emotional difficulties.

You transferred your own doubts and insecurities not only to Mitzy and Olaf, but also to Carlos and Carla and the other married Fellows. Luna tells me that you're going on Pill 2. I suggest that you start immediately; it will help you eliminate this kind of behavior from your interactions.

In addition, I suggest that you analyze your behavior patterns vis-a-vis people from other cultures. You tend to treat them as "culture types" and sources of cross-cultural information rather than individual personalities. I know from your computer-record that you have already half-perceived this pattern, but so far you have failed to act on this perception.

The question arises: how much did your behavior patterns contribute to our failure to develop an Owl Rock SITUATIONAL? This is an important question, because the answer may help you to rethink your behavior patterns during your interviews this year, and especially your choice of communication styles.

Given the realities which your departure has brought into being—and I must admit that it may turn out to be the best thing that could have happened—we will be holding a meeting in the near future for all those who have already discussed the need to change the format of the introduction-month. I'd personally be delighted if you'd come. I'm sure, however, that you've got too much to do for this to be wise this year. I hope you *will* be closely involved after your Fellowship year is over.

........**Record entry by Teg: re cross-cultural interaction** *(Document 13)*...

Morning, January 27, 1994

Luna wishes you "Light Luggage,"

Hassan

Conditions. Personally-controlled atmosphere. It's amazing how much more comfortable one's own carrel always is even though physical measurements of temperature, humidity, and purity show no difference from others.

Najo Hills has spoiled Quebec for me: before going there I thought that the Quebec environment was maximally supportive for me. Now

I discover that the far greater opportunities for being out in the
open air in Arizona are very attractive to me. I'm upset at myself,
though, for not taking sufficient advantage of them during January.
Personal attitude. I suppose I'm rather generally disappointed with
myself.

Text. While Luna and Hassan will be pleased that I've begun to
analyze my failure so rapidly, I'm not sure that I take much comfort in my father's remark that it takes chronological age to learn
from failure.

I was far too self-confident about my cross-cultural interaction before this time in Arizona. Although I can speak English and French
and three foreign languages, and although I'd experienced other
communities and I know all the thirty-year-old material about
"global villages" and "spaceship earth", it should have been obvious to me before that this was too little preparation for my year of
travel. I can't go into other communities and keep behaving as though
I were still home in Quebec. If my behavior-patterns remain the
same, simply trying to dress up like the community residents will
not change other peoples' perceptions of me.

If I'm to interact synergetically, I must inform myself about communities I shall be visiting this year. I can't do this by treating
a community resident as "typical" of his community culture
and questioning him on his behavior pattern. I must also stop
acting as though the reference point for understanding all other
communities is my own transcultural Quebec community and
its history. I must cease to assume that our founding myth is
more terranly synergetic, and therefore superior, compared to
other communities' founding myths. The Quebec myth of creating a maximally supportive environment for those in the Scientists Synergy who were creating the Invisible College was terranly synergetic fifteen years ago. But now the college is fully
functional and communities such as Najo Hills are doing work
which is more terranly necessary.

I shall have to pay special attention to behavior patterns which
are interpersonally sensitive, such as communication styles and ap-

pearance and consumption patterns. I already knew about the need for care in use of communication styles before going to Arizona. But when I was confronted with an actual need for cross-cultural inter-action, I still behaved as though my own SITUATIONAL could be used for communication. I also acted as though the Fellows would be "cultural types," not people with whom I should com-municate in a personal way. When I realized that finding an Owl Rock SITUATIONAL to encompass our communication needs would be highly time consuming, I justified my non-interaction as a need to concentrate on research and attributed my difficulties en-tirely to other people's failures.

Now I understand why everybody has been trying to convince me that the year will inevitably be tiring. I shall be living and inter-acting in communities which have their own life-styles—and which do not have many visitors. If I'm going to be able to synergize, I shall have to learn *their* SITUATIONAL, which, of course, really means understanding the life-style which is expressed in their communication styles. This will not be easy.

My plans for the year now seem very ambitious. I can see that I shouldn't have visited more than five people and I'm scheduled to see eight. I'm afraid that by the time I've learned enough SITUA-TIONAL to understand what is going on in each community it will be time to leave. I'm not willing to change my plans now, however.

I wonder how much of this new clarity follows from the fact that I took Hassan's advice and went on Pill 2 immediately. Luna was right. I only need two high-dresses, both in the Quebec-style: it's a relief to cut down on my baggage. I'm glad, in addition, that I'm going to stay on the North American continent for the next month because I need to rethink a great many of my preconcep-tions before I leave for China toward the end of February (par-ticularly those about consumption patterns.) I want to understand the socio-economic systems of the communities I visit, and I don't want to offend anybody with my consumption patterns. I must look again at the information on use of the terran credit cards: it will be difficult to learn to "buy" ecofacts after being used to obtaining them without any economic transaction.

Queries and Comments.

SECTION 11
LEARNING –
MONTHS TWO THROUGH SIX

........**Computer Summary Type 2 (with quotes) of interview** *Queries and*
by Teg with Historian, A *(Document 14)*....................... *Comments.*

February 18, 1994

(Teg's note: I have chosen to use a computer summary, type 2, (with quotes), to report my interviews with A, as I believe that this type of summary will best demonstrate the style of his interviews.)

Text. I consider that the critical period in modern history was between 1950 and 1980 and the major events either took place in the United States or were sparked from there.* Incidentally, this is one of the very few areas in which there is rather general world-wide agreement among historians. For better or worse, it was the power and idea-structures of the United States which dominated the currents of global development from the fifties through the seventies.

General Eisenhower was President of the United States during most of the fifties. At this time, a feeling developed that there was no need for major change in social and economic structures and institutions. Even intelligent social critics such as John Kenneth Galbraith basically agreed with this view. His book *The Affluent Society,* published in 1958, argued the need for major social changes, but essentially accepted that they were infeasible.

By the end of Eisenhower's second term in 1960, there had been a profound change in tone. President John F. Kennedy was elected—but only just—on a platform of "Let's get the country moving again." But neither the country nor the Congress really wanted change and just at the time when Kennedy had begun to rethink his strategy, he was assassinated.

> "If Kennedy had retained the Presidency, I am convinced
> that we would have avoided the disastrous events of the
> past twenty years, for there was a point in the mid-
> sixties when Kennedy's Brain Trust could have saved
> the country."

Queries and
Comments.

There was a large school which believed that the Kennedy assassination was not the work of a single deranged individual but rather
a conspiracy against the new frontiers proposed by Kennedy.
(Mark Lane became the best known representative of this school.)
If they were correct, there was never a clearer example of the
unexpected consequences of assassination. One result was that
the legislation which Kennedy could not pass was easily turned
into law by President Lyndon Johnson both in 1964, the year
immediately following the assassination, and also in 1965 and
1966, as a result of the overwhelming electoral victory of President Johnson in 1964.

The other result was a major escalation of the war in Vietnam.
There is considerable evidence that Kennedy had decided to re-
consider the direction in which policy was drifting in Southeast
Asia and to ensure that the war remained in the hands of the
South Vietnamese. President Johnson escalated the war until
well over half a million Americans were in Vietnam.

> "By 1968 America was totally off-balance. At this point
> the analysis among disaffected groups—with which I essen-
> itially agree—was that the university-military-industrial com-
> plex drifted into a war in Vietnam because it seemed imme-
> diately profitable and then de-escalated in 1969 and 1970
> because the war came to disrupt other, more crucial, estab-
> lishment goals. I have complete files of the underground
> press of this period, plus many 16 millimeter movies which
> document this view.

However, the war in Vietnam had set in motion several forces
which could not be contained and which eventually caused the
basic restructuring which has occurred in the United States and
throughout the world.

The black revolution
This emerged in the fifties and early sixties. Its original impetus
resulted from the courage of a few black individuals who recognized, and acted to remedy, conditions where they were not
receiving the rights which were automatically accorded to white
people. The literature of the movement is voluminous and illumin-

ating, ranging from the theoretical rhetoric of James Baldwin to the practical demands of such writers as Eldridge Cleaver.

In the halcyon days of the movement, black and white, young and old, demonstrated, picketed, and "sat down" together. The Washington March of 1963 remains for many an emotional high point in their lives, for it was perhaps the last time when it appeared that existing institutional structures were capable of accommodating to the changes required.

From this point on, the black movement began to divide and fragment. Two main movements developed: those who "wanted in" to the existing societal structures and those who recognized that only fundamental social change could provide all individuals with full human rights. The split was speeded and accentuated by the continuing assassinations of black and liberal leaders in the sixties.

The poor revolution

During and immediately after World War II, there was a temporary and basically spurious prosperity in the poor areas of the United States. With the return to a peace-time economy, this prosperity disappeared and the basic poverty of these areas returned. However, poverty was not considered a significant *social* problem at the end of the fifties, for it had been accepted that "the poor are always with us." The significance of poverty as a social problem was brought back to public attention through Michael Harrington's book, *The Other America,* and through the political stance developed by President Kennedy during the 1960 election.

Johnson's "War on Poverty", however, turned out to be a deception for almost all concerned. It started from the belief that the poor should be encouraged to participate, to the maximum possible extent, in the setting of policy. It rapidly became clear, however, that the policies of city hall and the interests of the poor were almost inevitably in conflict. Successive renewals of poverty programs therefore removed effective control ever further from the poor.

The Welfare Rights Movement emerged as the poor perceived

this development. Its efforts, plus inevitably rising welfare rolls resulting from growing problems of unemployability, brought about a major crisis in cities and states as the cost of welfare payments strained the capacity of available taxing methods. Some of the richer states, such as New York, even cut welfare payments at the time of rapid inflation at the end of the sixties. Even such improvements in benefit levels as were achieved were accompanied by increased bureaucratic intervention.

The poor naturally reacted with increased pressure, violence, and crime. Press, television, and movie coverage of these trends stimulated public indignation. The public response was a call for "law and order" rather than willingness to correct the intolerable conditions which existed.

The youth revolution

During the fifties the general complaint among adults who commented on "youth" was that they were the "silent generation." By the end of the sixties, most commentators would have chosen, if they could, to return to the fifties.

This youth revolution emerged from two major causes. First, a number of politicians caught the imagination of young people: President John Kennedy, Senator Eugene McCarthy, and Senator Robert Kennedy on the national scene, and several dynamic governors and mayors on the local and state levels. These young people who became involved in politics began to struggle for change; when they found the apparently available routes to change blocked by the cost of the Vietnam war, they were radicalized.

Second, the youth movement developed its own momentum because young middle-class whites ceased to be welcomed by most of those participating in the black and poor revolution and had to find their own direction. This led inevitably to a reconsideration of the relationship between teachers and students in schools and colleges and a growing attack on sterile patterns of learning.

The struggles for change in the seventies

"By the end of the sixties, most of the liberals who had been active in the three revolutions had chickened out. They had been happy to demand action so long as no action was demanded of them, but as soon as real change was called for they drew back. The radical movements found themselves increasingly isolated as the liberal-dominated mass-media withdrew support. The overwhelming pressure on all change agents then forced a new coalition whose nature was not clear till later. I and almost all my radical historian colleagues continued to describe the movement in terms of the black, the poor, and the young. We were not in the mood for intellectual analyses of on-going events—we felt that such spare time as we had should be given over to pamphleteering. Most of our days and nights were, however, spent participating in demonstrations and giving speeches to bring pressure on the more and more repressive establishment. In fact, I spent most of my time supporting those in jail or demanding the freedom of those in jail."

We can now see, however, that what appeared to be a joining of the young and the poor was actually an unexpected combination of the left, the right, and those who wished to revive the basic morality of the religious traditions. This should, perhaps, have been obvious at once, for all these groups had seen, in their own way, that the existing socio-economic system would not provide what they felt was required for a humane society. Thus the right wanted a return to traditional values, the left wanted to complete the socialist movement to more humane values, and there were an increasing number of people who wanted to return to a respect for the religious values. Each of these movements was demanding a society in which every person had the right to run his own life. Each of these groups recognized that this would only be possible in a society of self-restraint, rather than a society of coercively-imposed laws. Thus, they could make common cause against the bureaucracies which were increasingly limiting—and indeed destroying—the possibility of personal freedom.

"The Anti-Bureaucratic Coalition or ABC, as it came to be called, was formed in December 1970. There is a magnificent film-record on the initial mass meetings with television links between over half a million people in thirty cities. Many

blacks were active in the ABC, but there were others who remained convinced of the necessity of an all-black movement.

I am still shocked by the tactics of those who refused to
join us. Systems analysts and futurists shunned us on the
grounds that we were Utopian and naive, but this was obviously only an excuse for the replacement of necessary action by powerless words. Our political enemies claimed to
share our basic goals, but their actions showed they lied."

But ABC pressure coupled with the trends of the times soon
forced reorganization in the political line-up, which was profoundly different in 1972 than in 1968. President Nixon won in
1968 because the country wanted a change, but it was not until
the end of the 1968-1972 period that the direction of change became apparent.

Democratic and Republican party loyalty was heavily challenged
in 1969 by the patterns of local elections: a "law and order" candidate was able to win in many cities, regardless of party. While it
was originally assumed that this implied a "swing to the right" in
the old classic sense, it became clear in the Congressional elections of 1970 that there was a reaction against all thinking—regardless of party or political stance. People were assuming that
the answer to every problem, old or new, was a further government program (implying additional taxes and decreased personal
freedom).

Once the support for the revolt against big government and high
taxes was recognized, it brought about a profound restructuring
of the two political parties: a significant number of representatives,
senators, mayors and governors broke away from the Republicans and Democrats to form the Planning Party in mid-1971.

"I shall never forgive the treachery of a few of my fellow-
radicals who abandoned the ABC at this point and joined
the Planning Party. They distorted, for purposes of political
propaganda, the very arguments which we had intended to
use to bring pressure on the establishment. The Planning

Party argued that good planning would reduce the number of government programs, and therefore taxes, for there would be "one best way" (a phrase used by Jacques Ellul in his book *La Technique,* translated under the title *The Technological Society*) and that this one best way would be the cheapest. The ABC saw that when planning is carried out, bureaucracies inevitably grow, but we failed to put the point across."

The Planning Party won in 1972 with 28 per cent of the votes cast, the Democrats and Republicans split the remainder three ways with the George Wallace-approved candidate. Abstentions reached 40 per cent because the ABC had campaigned for abstention, arguing that none of the parties was relevant and that the political system should be attacked where possible, but ignored when this was impossible.

The Planning Party won because it had the most attractive representatives and senators as well as governors and mayors. It won because it was heavily financed: businessmen found its "efficiency" rhetoric close to what they understood. Finally the Planning Party won in 1972 because, in order to gain votes, it took over parts of the program of the ABC such as the guaranteed income and several decentralization measures. The leadership of the ABC was helpless to counter this tactic which reduced the percentage of absentions below that which had been hoped for. The same factor played the key role in the second electoral victory of the Planning Party in 1976.

"I have always thought the course of history might have been different if the radicals in the rich countries and the poor countries had coordinated their action-programs during the seventies. The ABC's justified concentration on personal freedom from bureaucratic action and its justified fear of fascism, left us with little time to worry about the economic concerns of the poor countries. We did not perceive the possibility that our *apparent* neglect (which was, of course, only a result of different priorities) would later lead to

*Queries and
Comments.*

a betrayal of the international radical movement by many
of those in the poor countries.

Even given our priorities, we might have spent more time
on the needs of the poor countries if we had not been heavily over-engaged in the States, and if the ABCs which
emerged later in Japan, Australia, and Europe, had not also
found their resources inadequate for the enormous task
they'd undertaken. Thus, although the ABC in the States set
up effective organization-structures which enabled us to win
many local victories, we never really moved toward our major goal of undermining bureaucracies throughout the
world."

The Presidential election of 1980

In 1979 our hopes were high again. The Planning Party would
have been in power for eight years by 1980 and democracies
have traditionally been averse to continuing a single party in
power for long periods. Confronted with the collapse of the Democratic and Republican Parties, the ABC decided—not without some
dissention—to run candidates in 1980. We felt it our duty to provide an effective opposition to the Planning Party, which would
otherwise win by default. We had concluded that it would be easier
to dismantle the bureaucratic system once we controlled it.

The 1979 Scientists Synergy, which demanded that public and private bureaucracies cease to withhold and distort information,
seemed at first sight to ensure our victory. We decided to adopt
this demand as our major election plank. Unfortunately, however,
for reasons which I have not yet been able to analyze, most of
the rank-and-file in the ABC left it during the course of the Scientists Synergy and supported their tactics and strategy, rather
than adhering to the plans which had been laid down by the
leadership of the ABC.

Because of these events, the ABC received only 25 per cent of
votes cast in the 1980 elections. The leadership of the ABC then
decided that reorganization was essential and the remaining hard-

core group, most of which had originally emerged from the left-wing and right-wing movements of the sixties, took on the name "Watchdogs." The Watchdogs have never really managed to be effective, largely due to their numerical weakness.

In recent years I've been giving increasing time to my studies. I'm now able to pass most evenings with my co-workers from the sixties and seventies and we recall events to make sure we lose none of the necessary data. We find film an invaluable witness for this purpose, as well as the records of the underground press.

"We are primarily studying the paradox that, although since 1980 we have less ability to put pressure on the establishment, there has been a rapid movement in the directions which the ABC and then the Watchdogs demanded. During recent years bureaucracies have been largely dismantled and the rights of local communities to make their own decisions have been fully established.

We are aware that the apparent correlation is being used to suggest that when pressure is reduced, crises are avoided and more effective change takes place. It is true that some indicators show that increasing rates of change *are* coupled with declining rates of pressure. However, I and my colleagues believe that other indicators show decreasing rates of change and we are working to explicate a theory to account for these phenomena.

We all remain convinced that the prime factor in the changes of the last thirty-five years has been the willingness of people to suffer, and even die, for the cause. We are sure that the relative calm of today in the rich countries augurs ill for the future.

........**Post-Comments by Teg on interviews with A, Historian**
(Document 15)..

Mid-morning, February 20, 1994

Conditions. All interviews with A took place in his study with
its book-lined walls, its tables littered with old newspapers and
reels of film scattered around the room. His communicator was
in an out-of-the-way storage-area because it "interfered with his
work." On several occasions I suggested ways in which print-outs
could be useful to us—they always came as a surprise to A.

A uses books, newspapers, pamphlets, audiotapes and, above all,
film, to illustrate his points. Every time we seemed to be settling
down and about to interact, he jumped up saying: "I've got evidence
to show this," and ran film from one of his many projectors.

He lives in Harlem, a community of some ninety thousand around
the old 125th Street of New York. Harlem was the "black center"
of North America for several decades. A lives there not because
he's comfortable, but in order to "prevent a total separation of the
races." I tried to suggest that if people from one race or one
cultural origin wanted to live together in Harlem or in any other
community they had a right to make this choice.

A's view was that although residents of abundance-regions should
be allowed to freely exercise their choice of living in mono-cul-
tural, multi-cultural, or transcultural communities, every community should always contain residents from other communities so
that complete and irreversible cultural divergence would not
take place. I argued that surely the existence of transcultural
communities would prevent this. A said "no" because they were really
neo-cultural communities, in the process of forming a culture of their
own.

Reflecting on our argument, I now think that we were both wrong. *Queries and*
I was wrong about the transcultural communities forming a *Comments.*
bridge to the future. (I'm sure now that, while they may be internally synergetic, they are not necessarily terranly synergetic.)
A was wrong about permanent extra-community residence being
the way to prevent irreversible divergence, because this is just
coercion in disguise. I wonder how, and if, irreversible cultural divergence *can* be avoided?

Personal attitude. Exasperated with myself. I brought this month on
myself, against the advice of other historians I know. I'd read some
of the material which A had put out on the sixties and it seemed to
me he had some valid insights—I still think so.

I had hoped to get a summary of the events of recent decades seen
from the North American point of view. I got what seemed to me to
be a biased, emotionally-colored series of anecdotes (I instructed
the computer to delete these) joined by a barely perceptible thread
of connecting events described mostly in OUTER (these were brought
out by the computer summary).

I've wondered, following Hassan's warning to me, whether I didn't
give A the wrong perception of what I wanted from my interviews
with him. But then I remembered the pattern of the whole month
and realized that this couldn't possibly have been the case. For
example, A continued to use film to "prove" points even though
I showed him again and again that film could be biased and was
easily distortable.

Of course, A hadn't the advantage of those now in the third life-
period which comes from being taught about techniques of audio
and visual perception distortion. I find it difficult to remember
how much learning is available to us as compared to people now
in the fourth life-period. One of the classic distortion tricks, of
course, is to use just the video of a film and add voice-over and
music. I remember one example with a Latin American street
setting.

The video portion of the film showed a youth carrying a package,

shouting excitedly up to another leaning out of a window above.
In the distorted version, "riot" music had been added. The com-
mentator explained that the pressure of hunger was leading to
widespread troubles throughout South America, and that in this
scene a youth carrying a wrapped pistol was urging another to
join him in street rioting. The film was then run through again
with the actual audio: the youth was telling his friend that he had
to take a package of protein-enriched flour to his grandmother
before coming to play cards.

A obviously glories in the fact that he lived in the industrial era
and took part in the violence and disruption of the sixties and
seventies. It is clear that his life really ended around 1980 and
that he is now attempting to relive it with his "fellow-radicals."
For example, whenever one of their friends' or enemies' faces appeared on the screen during evening viewing sessions, they stopped
the film and played "whatever-happened to?"

That's not their only game. They also play "what-might-have-
been"; apparently A and his group haven't even realized that
each decision removes the possibility of all alternative futures
which might have emerged if a different decision had been made.
We played "what-might-have-been" at the age of five and six to
encourage imagination and were then considered to have out-
grown any possible benefit from it.

It seems to me that I have wasted much of my first two months.
I know from my Arizona experience that it is possible to learn
from failure, but it remains true that more is learned from success.
I'm going to take two days in the Virginia Coast National Park to
see if I can discover what I'm doing wrong. I must also decide
what report I should make on A's level of competence. I think I
know what I should do, but I find it difficult to accept the responsibility.

Text. From beginning to end of my interviews with A he was advancing interpretations of events with which I disagreed, but the
statement with which I most disagreed was contained in the last
quote of the computer summary. A believes in the "willingness of peo-

ple to suffer, and even die, for the cause." I learned the grafitti: "Nobody is more entropic than the willing martyr."

Queries and Comments.

I thought that everyone was agreed (once again I discover that present dialogue-focusers fail to reflect the full range of views) that the origins of the sixties-confusion, the deterioration into a seventies-entropy, and the upturn into the eighties-synergy were clearly perceptible. The agreed view starts from the concept that, historically, cultures continued to develop so long as they created new groups with new ideas relevant to the new conditions which were emerging. These new groups could then struggle their way to the top and bring about adaptions in the total socioeconomic system. When a culture failed to make change in leadership possible, it collapsed. While such collapses were profoundly disruptive, they were part of a process which ensured the continuation of human history.

In the sixties, this ancient process of change finally broke down. During the years following World War II, those in power in both the "rich" regions and the "poor" regions had decided to stabilize all systems which were under their control: to prevent change in international frontiers, to minimize economic disruptions, to limit insurrections. For the first time, such decisions could be implemented with increasing expectation of success, because of the new technologies.

This deliberate policy of blocking traditional change-routes unbalanced both national and international socioeconomic systems. For example, the avoidance of slumps over twenty-five years ensured that the international exchange system was badly imbalanced by the late sixties and also that many industries continued to exist even though they had become socially entropic and were no longer fulfilling any real economic need.

By the beginning of the seventies, the policy of preventing socioeconomic and political adaption had been implemented so fully that both socioeconomic and political systems had become dangerously rigid. There was an increasing risk of breakdown in the functioning of bureaucratic systems because, so long as they con-

Queries and tinued to act bureaucratically, they were unable to respond to the
Comments. reality of outside conditions.

Some bureaucracies were responding to the challenge by trying to decrease their rigidity and organizing more informally. Increasingly, decisions were taken by an informal communication net which functioned on the basis of sapiential authority based on knowledge rather than structural authority based on position. But informal communication nets require a climate of trust for their existence and continued growth: the socioeconomic conditions at the beginning of the seventies were unfavorable for such a development.

The forming of the ABC in 1970 accelerated the trend toward scrutiny and criticism of bureaucratic structures. Even those to whom ABC tactics were most repellent found themselves more than half-convinced by the argument for applying pressures on bureaucracies in order to curb their monolithic tendencies. In particular, the media waged a permanent campaign against "Big-Brother-Bureaucratic Decisions. The heads of bureaucracies, who had discovered that the process of delegation produced better decisions, were actually prevented from moving in this direction by the inaccurate, sensational, mass-media coverage of the time.

Contrary to A's beliefs, the agreed view is that the ABC's tactics contributed heavily to the entropy of the seventies. While it was certainly necessary to bring pressure on the bureaucracies at the beginning of the sixties in order to create self-consciousness among those with power, the continuation of pressure in the seventies, when everybody and every organization was always off-balance, was severely entropic. It began to be feared, at the beginning of the seventies, that it would be impossible to make intelligent decisions because of the degree of confusion throughout the world. The final result of continuing revolutionary pressure would therefore be the destruction of the carrying capacity of the earth, either through total war or through the continuing degradation of the environment.

Nobody seems to fully understand the processes by which we

emerged from the seventies-entropy, but considerable emphasis *Queries and*
is usually given to two growing synergies: *Comments.*

   1. People became aware that it was reasonable to perceive the world as being in breakdown and that the difficulties in their personal lives were the result of the overall
   entropic situation and not of their own failure. A new word
   was coined to describe this, amondie. Once the concept of
   amondie was understood, the opposing concept of anomie—
   that one was failing to find one's role in a society assumed
   to be functioning successfully—fell into disuse.

   2. Small teams of people began to research the procedures
   and methods by which accurate movement of information
   could be ensured. Several study groups were created and
   communication nets grew up relating synergetic people and
   ensuring effective coordination of their work. This laid part
   of the basis for the 1979 Scientists Synergy.

The convergence of the Scientists Synergy and the Planning Party
in late 1979, coupled with new patterns of communication and
public awareness of the need for major change, made possible increasing synergy throughout the eighties.

Upon reflection and comparison, I can see no validity in A's interpretation of the events of 1979/80. Perhaps I'll change my
mind when I hear B's account of the Scientists Synergy in a few
days.

........**Letter from Ben, Teg's Recommender for Orwell Fellowship, to Teg: re Teg's reaction to A, Historian** *(Document 16)*..

Evening, February 20, 1994

Conditions. Computer-ideal under the dome, as always. I'm too old
for winter sports and I'm getting a feeling that nothing ever changes
here. I thought I was settled for life and that this need for change

Queries and
Comments.

had been left behind me. Is it worth finding out if other people would like to get rid of the dome? Should I think about moving?

Personal attitude. A little regretful for you, but encouraged.

Text. You'll get yourself a complex if you're not careful. I know this language is old-fashioned, but because of my date of birth and upbringing it's deep in me, and when I'm comfortable with somebody it tends come out. You can certainly convert it into present INTER.

Yes, your introduction-month was a failure, although Hassan now seems to feel that you acted as the catalyst for already-thought-through-change rather than forcing a mutation. *No, you didn't fail during your second month:* admittedly your choice of historian was wrong, but once you met him your reaction was constructive and your comments on his view show that you've learned. His world-view is so negative that you should *not* be able to enter into it. Only his own historian-colleagues need to understand his point of view at this time.

You've no right to concern yourself with A's reputation. Remember "Smithy." When he was called in to facilitate at Aldrinton, just over the hill from us, he destroyed the community because of his lack of competence. When we checked back on his record, we discovered that he'd failed several times before but nobody had wanted to hurt him; so he was put in a situation where he broke up a community of 75,000 people. You're discovering early the responsibility of being in the Invisible College. We all go through it.

Ben

........**Information Print-Out: Abundance-Region Terran Credit Card: Used in Scarcity Regions** *(Document 17)*.................

Compiled January 1993

Production and consumption patterns vary according to region and community. The following should be noted:

Queries and Comments.

1. **Sociofacts** (goods and services resulting from non-structured activities.) These are community-produced and are distributed according to the custom of each community; therefore visitors cannot use their credit cards to obtain sociofacts in any community.

2. **Ecofacts** (goods and services resulting from structured activities.) Ecofact production is adequate to meet auto-estimated needs in abundance regions. Credit cards are therefore no longer in use in abundance-regions.

   Note. A limited number of communities in abundance-regions are committed to sensory overload. In these circumstances, as there is no theoretical limit to demand for ecofacts, money is used as a medium of exchange. Visitors to these communities must therefore use credit cards to obtain ecofacts.

Ecofact production is not yet adequate to meet needs in the scarcity regions. Residents of abundance-regions travelling in scarcity regions should therefore use their terran credit cards to obtain their auto-estimated needs of ecofacts.

Note. Abundance-region residents are reminded that the abundance regions of the world are still considered to bear the responsibility for the continuing existence of scarcity, Commitment to terran solidarity by the abundance-regions in the thirty-five years following World War II would have ensured abundance throughout the world at the present time. Although conditions are improving through increased transfer of ecofacts from the abundance-regions to the scarcity-regions, there is a cultural limit on rate of absorption. Consumption is restricted in scarcity-regions by use of the community credit-card; its value varies according to community and role-class; this community credit-card is generally valid throughout the scarcity-regions. Scarcity-region residents travelling in abundance regions are not, of course, restricted in obtaining ecofacts.

........Main points of introductory statement by B, Scientist, with pre-comments by Teg *(Document 18)*......................

Midday, March 5, 1994

Conditions. People. Hardly an original comment and one that I shouldn't feel driven to make in light of the population data. China, like most of the scarcity-regions, still has a net rise in population, although it's negligable. But the sharp drop in the birth rate only came ten years ago and the need for housing and community buildings remains critical. The need is increased by the fact that they don't have anything like the Najo Hills Multihogan here; housing is still separate from community buildings and the latter are therefore still only used for limited parts of the day. The question in this area is how to establish co-residence patterns which maximize the benefits available from limited land availability and to help people discover which types of community will be .best for them.

Personal attitude. I'm less emotional. I'd like to feel that I'm making peace with myself in my relationship with the Invisible College, but I know from my latest computer-record medical compilation that several changes are due to Pill 2. I hate the feeling that my attitudes are being altered by chemicals, but it is clear to me that even *with* the pill I'm only just able to function—I must continue with it.

Two preoccupations are conflicting for emotional attention. I've sent off my tel on A's competence. It's a zero because, of course, I have no right to send anything else. On the other hand, I'm looking forward to talking with B here. He's corresponded with father who, in fact, suggested I should meet him. He's got a competence criteria of 9.5. (I believe that nobody has ever achieved more than a 9.6 out of a theoretical maximum of 10.) Perhaps more importantly, he's obviously going to be willing to spend considerable time with me, as well as to encourage the best of his apprentices to talk with me.

I hope that they will remember not to use their science INTER to me. Although father is a scientist, I've never really been involved. Until I was 18 or so I was more interested in the feminine swing away from being a surrogate man toward an emphasis on being a "woman." This was partly due to mother and the roles she played in the seventies' neo-Luddite revolt against machine-systems and in the consumers' revolt: she saw them as ways of preventing women from being turned into sex symbols for encouragement of purchasing. I'm now outgrowing my mother's priorities but they have limited my interest in the sciences. I must acquire a clearer understanding of the role of science. (Indeed, I still perceive scientists as working in laboratories; I really should internalize the fact that computers and robots do nearly all the experiments.) B asked me if I'd like an overall summary. I felt it would be useful and I was right. I've just been rereading the main points.

Text. I was one of the first young people who were permitted to leave China for study. I'd intended to be away for four years, but was away for seven. It wasn't till 1984 that China supported the 1979 Scientists Synergy.

I'd been at Jodrell Bank, the British astronomical center, as an apprentice for two years when the news services announced in February 1979 that a widespread epidemic had started in Africa as a result of the employment of germ warfare by European mercenaries. The possibility of this danger had been a subject of heated debate among the public ever since a 1969 United Nations report.

One week later, a number of young scientists around the world published a manifesto stating that the only hope for the survival of the world was the full use of all the available scientific knowledge. This is generally seen as the real beginning of the Scientists Synergy. They drew attention to the suppression of information about existing systems of chemical, biological, and radiological weaponry. They announced that the need for complete honesty in information transfer was now so great that they would no longer participate in either suppressing or distorting information to fit the needs of their public or private employers.

The young group of scientists, having published their manifesto, proceeded rapidly to act upon it. Crucial secret industrial processes with potential to considerably increase food production, if adapted for this purpose, were released. Classified government reports, which contradicted published government findings, were made available. The draft statements of think-tanks, funded by outside sources, were published with annotations showing important changes which had been made later and which clearly favored those funding the report. In addition, a careful and intelligent campaign was started to inform the public that these well-known patterns of information-distortion were only the tip of the iceberg—that adverse data was not usually included even in the first draft of a report because what was expected of the report was made clear before it was funded.

Reactions to the Scientists Synergy varied from nation to nation. Authorities in countries with strong theoretical beliefs in freedom of information movement reacted cautiously. Authorities in others prosecuted immediately both for "Releasing Official Secrets." As only young scientists, without prestige and in subordinate positions, were involved, it became clear that even in the countries where the initial reactions had been cautious, strong suppressive action would soon be taken.

As so often happens, the action of these young scientists forced the hand of the more hesitant group. The senior scientists had long recognized that a showdown over the question of freedom of information movement was inevitable, but their tendency had been to put off action as long as possible arguing that trends were running in favor of change.

Following the publication of the manifesto, inconclusive discussions continued among senior scientists until the international group of scientists at Jodrell Bank announced their decision to participate in the Scientists Synergy in April. During the following week the

names of those announcing their participation would have made
a world-wide Who's Who of the physical sciences—participation of
those in the social sciences was far more limited.

The pattern in the scarcity-regions was very different from that in
the abundance-regions. Governments in the scarcity-regions needed
the very few of their scientists who had not been attracted to the
abundance-regions by the higher salaries and apparently greater
work opportunities available. But their need did not result in greater comprehension of the significance of the synergy re-organization
principles for the total society. Many scarcity-region governments
had not even begun to understand the principle of sapiential authority which was the organizing mechanism of the Scientists Synergy. In those cases where the scientists were able to argue the potential for economic development inherent in free information
movement, governments supported the Scientists Synergy; in those
cases where governments only perceived a limitation of their power,
they acted against it.

But the actions of the scarcity-region governments were not decisive
in the final outcome of the Scientists Synergy. It was determined by
the actions in the abundance-regions. Those in charge of government, intellectual, and industrial bureaucracies found themselves
in a dilemma. Governments and marketives could dismiss all those
who refused to observe secrecy policies, but this would force them
to get rid of people whom they needed in order to function
effectively.

Given this reality, some organizations tried to destroy the morale
of the Scientists Synergy by dismissing subordinate personnel;
but they discovered that if they dismissed or disciplined subordinates,
all those participating in the Scientists Synergy would leave. Thus
any move made by organizations automatically led to the loss of
all those personnel who were most valuable to them.

Nevertheless, during the first half of 1979, a number of organizations implemented a policy of punitive dismissals. This brought
about a rethinking and reorganization of the Scientists Synergy.
Some scientists, like your father, sought maximally supportive en-

vironments in which to interact to create the Invisible College, while some joined organizations which supported the manifesto. By the end of 1979 there had been a significant restructuring of organizations directly employing scientists.

An emergency fund was established by the scientific community to support those scientists who were dismissed; an individual who was dismissed received one hundred percent of the income required for his auto-estimated needs until he found a new job: this was easily financed by a ten percent contribution from all those participating in the Scientists Synergy who still held their jobs. (After the Scientists Synergy was accepted, many scientists continued to contribute from one to five percent of their income to this fund, which was then used to support work toward terran citizenship.)

The outcome of the Scientists Synergy hung in the balance for a time. A surprising number of social scientists—particularly those in political science—supported efforts to suppress the Synergy. The public, which was increasingly inconvenienced, tended to follow the social sciences and the media. The media in turn usually followed the views of those who provided its revenues rather than the policy which would have appeared logical from its theoretical code in favor of free information movement.

In the end, the balance was held by the ABCs in the abundance-regions. I was pessimistic about the stands they would take because of my reactions following their cooperation with the neo-Luddite revolt. This revolt of the seventies, which justified the destruction of machinery and machine-systems, gained most of its strength from the public's distrust of scientists. A significant segment of public opinion came to believe that not only were science and technology creating many of the problems currently plaguing societies, but that there were also no effective techniques to deal with the situations which were being created.

You should realize that the material destruction of machines during the neo-Luddite revolt provided the final disillusionment for many revolutionaries in the scarcity-regions. When we perceived the close cooperation between the Neo-Luddites and the ABCs throughout

the abundance-regions, we came to realize that there could be little
international collaboration among radicals. Those who claimed to
identify with our needs were participating in the destruction of machines and machine-systems which could have been used to provide
the food, clothing, and shelter we so urgently required.

It appeared by mid-1979 as though my worst fears about the role
of radicals in abundance-regions were going to be justified. The
various ABCs tried to co-opt the Scientists Synergy. They were un-
successful because, like many bureaucracies, they failed to understand that the organizing principle of the Scientists Synergy was
sapiential authority. The ABCs had adopted the most rigid bureaucratic practice—although they claimed to be struggling against
them. In the end, the ABCs neither acted against the Scientists
Synergy nor supported it; they merely attempted to profit from it.

It was at this juncture that a decisive intervention was made by the
radical movements in the scarcity-regions. They acted to widen a
split which had been developing throughout the seventies between
the leadership and the rank and file of the ABCs in the abundance-
regions. The leadership of the ABCs was increasingly drawn from
hard-core former left- and right-wingers whose methods were pressure tactics and disruption; but its rank and file, particularly the
young and the women, were coming to understand the implications
of recent research on mechanisms of thought. It was shown that
change in thought patterns could only be achieved by creating new
perceptions and stress was proved disruptive, thereby decreasing
the possibility of new perceptions. The tactics of the ABCs were
therefore seen as counterproductive by a growing number of the
rank and file.

The break between the leaders and the membership developed first
in the United States in late summer of 1979. The leadership of the
ABCs there suddenly found itself largely without followers, while
the Scientists Synergy had gained effective, immediate understanding and support from the most dynamic young people and
women in the culture. At this point, the Planning Party, which
recognized the precariousness of its position in terms of the 1980
elections, was forced by events to adopt the goals of the Scientists

*Queries and
Comments.*

Queries and
Comments. Synergy. It moved rapidly and decisively to accept and promote the free information principles contained in the manifesto and began to replace structural authority with sapiential authority.

Of course the activity which most people associate with the Scientists Synergy is the understanding and development of new communications-styles. Efforts started with INTER. At the time of the manifesto, we had thought that deliberate distortion was the only barrier to effective socio-political communication. Afterward we came to believe that the real communication barrier was in imprecision of terms used by politicians.

We hoped to create for the politican a set of terms which would be as unambiguous as that used by the physical sciences. We originally built upon the computer languages of the sixties and seventies and on the specialized languages of the physical and social sciences. Progress was slow. We found it necessary to get rid of many socio-political terms commonly accepted as "exact" because they were derived from the social sciences and were part of a terminology which was esoteric rather than explicative, i.e., the jargon was designed to keep out the uninitiated rather than clarify issues.

When INTER had emerged and was being perfected, its uses proved to be very narrow. The very fact that the words and terms were unambiguous reduced the unexpected occurrence of potentially insightful—if often immediately inaccurate statements—during conversations. For example, "noise", which is the source of new innovations in communication, was progressively banished. Those who used INTER were therefore more and more effective in the solution of already-defined problems and the recall of already-found solutions, and less and less effective in recognizing that accepted definition and analysis of a situation might be inadequate and that conceptual and semantic reworking was necessary.

We had aimed to create more logical patterns for socio-political communication and we had ended up with INTER, a communication-style which was not appropriate for examining emerging difficulties. We attained, however, something which we had not expected; INTER made it possible to examine, on the basis of strict rules of logic, any subject for which goals and conditions were already known and could be clearly stated. This logical communications style made it possible to carry on all deductive processes by the use of computers.

Queries and Comments.

A few scientists had been aware from the beginning that the creation of INTER would not achieve our goals. Rather than spending their time trying to convince those working on INTER, they started to study what was later called OUTER: the verbal process by which new insights are discovered.

OUTER is used quite differently from INTER. In OUTER discussion, individuals voice thoughts which they do not even understand fully themselves; the whole group then tries to discover the implications of what has been stated. If the group has achieved the required level of trust, remarkable progress can be made in achieving new perceptions and in creating new realities.

The first result of gaining understanding of the INTER and OUTER communication-styles was to decrease rapidly the number of discussions which could not be productive because some of those present were talking in INTER and some in OUTER.

However, OUTER too is very limited in its utility for it can only be employed if it is useful to abandon all preconceptions and to follow ideas wherever they lead. While this is often desirable in research, it is inappropriate and disruptive in most real-life situations.

In the mid-eighties, communities were in the process of creation and re-creation all over the world and a new communication difficulty had become apparent. Outsiders with special skills were everywhere attempting to interact with community residents in order to facilitate community development. But special INTER vocabularies accompanied the special skills and residents were bored or irritated by outsiders who attempted to clarify ideas on community needs by holding explorative OUTER sessions. If there was no shared culture, there was no basis for mutual understanding and trust.

Queries and Comments.

Subsequent analysis of successful interactions showed that:

> 1. Emphasis had shifted from the speaker to the listeners. INTER precision of presentation or OUTER richness of thought had been replaced by a concern for appropriate presentation.

> 2. In order to make an appropriate presentation, the speaker had to share a purpose with his listeners. Communities, consentives, families, or other groups function because they share a culture; they have accepted a set of purposes (which may be implicit) and conventions which are respected in all situations.

> 3. Presentation was carefully adjusted to the specific situation, general conditions, personalities of people present, etc.

This communication-style therefore came to be called SITUATIONAL. This is the only communication-style in which interaction in ongoing situations can be successful. Such interaction must accept the current reality as the starting point and ensure minimum disruption; nothing that already exists or has been decided should be changed without necessity. Every change takes time and energy which could be used for individual and community growth. *If changes are essential they must be clearly announced so that all concerned can be aware of them.*

SITUATIONAL includes INTER vocabulary for those aspects of community life which already exist (and which will continue unless directly challenged.) INTER for such purposes permits effective shorthand and saving of time. Many communities have their own supplements to the general computer INTER dictionaries. SITUATIONAL also includes OUTER to permit discussions of change, although no community considers it necessary to continuously challenge all the activities based on the arbitrary conventions of the culture.

The area where most of my apprentices are working is on the

psycho-social implications of the ongoing redefinition of life-and-death. They are moving beyond my competence and I expect them to leave the apprentice relationship and create their own Institute very shortly—a long overdue development for this p/p area. You'll learn most by talking to my apprentices directly, but before you do, a brief summary of the implications may be helpful.

Queries and Comments.

It became clear in the early seventies that multi-generational hereditary malfunctions were in fact very rare and that post-natal, childhood, and adult conditions of ill-health were a function of the environment in which the individual or his parent lived. But so long as the cultural patterns of the industrial era continued, it was inevitable that most people would live in environmental conditions which were injurious to their health.

The concept of "health" was completely redefined in the abundance-regions during the socio-economic reorganization following the Scientists Synergy. Medicine had already discovered the cure for most diseases but there were not the medical personnel to ensure that the new curative techniques benefitted all the population. To lessen the load, governments created programs of preventive medicine by setting up diagnostic computer centers. An unanticipated finding of those working with the resulting data was that the program of curative medicine could be largely replaced by a program of promotive medicine.

As programs of promotive medicine developed, the concept of health was redefined again as "the pattern which provides an individual with the greatest possibility to maximize his potentials." The environmental needs for each person's self-maximization change with chronological age and if patterns of living are adjusted to these needs it is possible to continue maximization of potentials until senility.

Senility had ceased to be automatically regarded as a pre-death state early in the 1950's. During that decade it began to be possible to retain a heart-beat, and even evidence of brain function, long after the indivudal had ceased to exist as a personality. In order to deal with the reality that death today is "chosen" by most

Queries and
Comments.

people, rather than imposed by a failure of physical functioning, we have internalized the existentialist insight that everything that is not in the process of being born is in the process of dying.

........Record entry by Teg: re high-evening by the Great Wall
(Document 19)...

After midnight, March 28, 1994

Conditions. My personal room in the community guest house.

Personal attitude. It's been a wonderful month. I learned to live in a community which has totally different behavior patterns from anything I've ever experienced, and managed to understand their SITUATIONAL rather than attempting to communicate in mine. I even attained, on certain days, the attitude which made their four-times-daily calisthenics promotive of health.

I'm over my fear that I won't be able to interact in any of the communities which I'll be visiting this year. It would have been very easy to ruin this month also if I'd not applied some of the skills which I'd learned since the beginning of my Orwell Fellowship.

I found that I was enjoying my interviews with B, although I didn't understand all his thoughts and some of his evaluations of historical events were different from any I'd heard before. In view of mother's role, his negative reaction to the neo-Luddite revolt was a real shock to me. I was very interested in B's version of why the Anti-Bureaucratic Coalition broke up. A real contrast to A's.

I've wondered on several occasions what would have happened if A and B ever got together.

Text. The apprentices and I were out this evening for a farewell high-meal. The celebration-hall overlooks the Great Wall. A week

ago we went up to make our reservations and explained our reason for coming; we worked out what we should wear with the
decor planner and gave our ideas about what we might eat. High
meals in B's community are considered socio-facts: each resident
is expected to contribute to making the celebration-hall synergetic
and is entitled to eat there when they wish.

*Queries and
Comments.*

The decor planner was extraordinarily successful: the lights,
banners, and the costumes of the participants all combined to
make a whole of extraordinary beauty. It was difficult to remember that the gestalt was unique for the evening. I'd chosen
a traditional Chinese costume from the high-dresses in the
Community-Store and it was one of the few times in my life
I was glad to be small, for otherwise I'd have been forced to
wear one of my Quebec high-dresses I'd brought with me. Luna
was right. The girls certainly seemed to enjoy dressing me
up in their community costume.

The atmosphere was particularly welcoming, for the apprentices had not only eaten here before but had often served meals
as their contribution to the celebration-hall. It is clearly important to the community that the celebration-hall is maintained by sociofact contributions and that credit cards cannot
be used here.

Our meal ended with what is locally known as the Firework Liquor.
Its title seemed completely justified, perhaps partly because I, like
almost all those now in the third life-period, only drink at celebrations. We then had a fireworks display which seemed to fill the
heavens, but which was, of course, only an extraordinarily effective computer light-program.

Suddenly, about half-way through the evening, I realized that
although this was one of the most successful celebrations I'd
ever attended I wasn't getting the fun out of it I expected.
And then I understood that this was the direct result of Pill 2
and wished I'd gone off it for at least a few days. Then I
perceived that this wouldn't have worked either because I have
become so attached to the group here that I couldn't have left
without emotional disruption.

Dearpeers,

After breakfast, April 14, 1994 (Betty's birthday. Best wishes.)

Conditions. Calcutta is very depressing! There was population pressure in the part of China from where I have just come, but there was no social breakdown. I didn't see Shanghai, of course, but it's apparently in exactly the same situation as Calcutta.

Effective, culturally-acceptable contraceptives for Asia were developed so late that the size of population cohorts only stabilized around 1984. Cultures collapsed in many areas and people were increasingly driven to the urban areas as the least bad of the available possibilities. Calcutta today is a conglomerate of twenty-five million people: efforts to reconstruct functioning communities within Calcutta fail through sheer weight of numbers.

Emigration to Australia, Africa, and North America is beginning to make a difference, but very slowly. Even the most optimistic see the year 2000 as the date for the beginning of real progress; those who have been attempting community facilitation for decades seem to have given up hope.

Since arriving in Calcutta I've begun to understand fully the extent of the tensions caused by restrictions on travel and emigration to abundance-regions. This wasn't obvious in B's community in China because the residents find their environment supportive. Ecofact availability is rising rapidly there and any remaining shortages are more than compensated by a highly synergetic community myth and the consequent wide availability of desired sociofacts.

Few, however, would want to stay here in Calcutta if they had *any* alternative, however unsatisfactory. Provision of ecofacts from the abundance-regions is satisfying minimal needs, but the absence of any opportunity to improve personal or family conditions deepens the pervasive despair. Sociofact production is, of course, rare in these conditions. Under these circumstances, the possibility of emigration is the sole remaining hope for those who have initiative.

Personal attitude. It's a long way from home. I'm learning, but I'm tired. Now I *know* why people told me the year would be difficult.

Text. I must share what I've just learned with somebody and it had better be somebody of my own age. During yesterday's facilitation session with C, I learned about the "education system" of the sixties. If I tell anyone who was "at school" then how entropic it was, they may feel attacked.

After the session with C, one of the apprentices here and I were having a relaxed evening. We'd set the computer on random search among sixties-films on the first three life-periods. We discovered a behavior-pattern which amazed us: during the sixties protest about educational conditions was expressed in a way which could not possibly have been expected to bring about change.

I'm sure I've been told about this reality in a dozen different ways, but somehow I never really got inside the system before listening to C. During the sixties it appears that *only one form of "education"* was valued—"authoritarian teaching" and "rote assimilation of materials" inside schools for those up to eighteen and inside colleges for those up to 22 (and in many cases beyond.)

Schools and colleges contained large numbers of "students" who were taught in classes of up to forty in schools and as many as a thousand or more in colleges. This size of class was considered practical because people were expected to rote-memorize what previous scholars had taught and then reinform the teacher about existing theories. Apparently no one expected that students would retain the knowledge beyond the "exam" period designed to test people for recent-information-recall.

I can't make sense of this pattern. If the object had been to train people in a specific skill, classes of this size would have been a possible technique, given the fact that auto-training with computers and robots did not exist at that time. But then those involved would have continued practicing the same skill until it became automatic and their constant need for the skill would have ensured that it was retained. Tests to discover information-recall would have been unnecessary. On the other hand, if the object was education, a repeated forcing of existing concepts on the student would prevent him from internally rearranging the information into new patterns and perceiving new insights, which is the function of any effective educational process.

In the sixties the confusion about appropriate techniques of learning was not apparently due to any lack of concern. In addition, the films we saw made it clear that many of those involved in education as teachers and learners saw that the entire educational system was dysfunctional. But those who protested didn't seem to have any idea of the way in which change is achieved. They held "rallies" and "sit-ins" protesting the actual detailed functioning of the educational system without recognizing that changes in part of a system are not possible without changing the total system, and that it is not possible to change total systems unless those involved comprehend a changed perception of the nature of the universe.

The increasing disruption and violence which accompanied student "rallies" and "sit-ins" during the late sixties set in motion two forces which led to the collapse of many government and private universities. First, private donors and government agencies cut back on the funds they supplied. Second, an increasing number of young people no longer saw college as essential to their life-development and sought alternative patterns of learning.

By the mid-seventies, college and universities were attempting to develop programs which would attract both new donors and students. It was unfortunate that many of the colleges which had the clearest comprehension of the new approach to learning, and which were therefore able to attract students, did not have the merchandising skills to attract funds. By the end of the seventies, a large proportion of colleges and universities had disbanded.

In a few cases, the buildings of a college or university were purchased by groups of individuals who created new forms of communities in which learning was an integral part of the community style: the sharp age-breaks between those learning and those working began to disappear. These new institutions and those colleges which did survive moved in one or two directions; they became either local or transnational nodes in the de-Chardinian noosphere. As such, they acted as transmission points for information.

The local nodes began to develop ways in which they could serve their immediate community. These local organizations used, among other innovations, patterns of learning interaction developed by the Street Universities and also brought in by individuals from India and other nations with traditions of personal facilitation. They were able to demonstrate how real education could take place within the community rather than cut off from it in schools and colleges.

In the second case, when institutions and colleges moved toward being transnational nodes in the noosphere, they concentrated increasingly in a single p/p area. It was made clear to those who wished to join these emerging institutions that their purpose was to elucidate a specific p/p area and that nobody should seek admission if they were not interested in this area of knowledge. As this process of moving toward being a transnational node continued, it was understood that information structured around p/p areas required new forms of presentation. It became necessary to replace these methods which had been used for deduction and transfer of data within "disciplines," such as rote-learning texts and personal interpretation of facts written by an "authority" for his followers. The continuing transformation of transnational nodes later converged with the

Queries and Comments.

Queries and Comments. efforts of those who were interacting, following the Scientists Synergy, to create the Invisible College and the p/p Institutes.

I see that I've got, as usual, way beyond what I intended to write. But I'd never understood till I talked to C that the learning pattern we take for granted was so recent in origin. Nor had I realized the irony of the present degenerated state of Indian education, in view of the fact that the traditional Indian attitude toward education contributed so much to the beginnings of present learning patterns in the abundance-regions.

C is working on the reorganization of the Indian learning process along traditional lines. Given the evolution of educa-tion in the abundance-regions, she is able to use the present abundance-region techniques. The communicators and other equipment are plentifully available, but there are very few here who understand how to facilitate. C has established a program for educational facilitators and she suggested that I look at the outline of the introductory film to see the elementary level at which she has had to begin.

I wish I were going to see you before November.

Forward,

Teg

........Outline of introductory film prepared for apprentices by C, Education Facilitator *(Document 21)*......................

THE LEARNING PROCESS (created November 1993)

(Level 5, Full Color, Photography and Animation, English, Language, Musical Background, Time 10 Minutes.)

NO. OF SECONDS	AUDIO	VIDEO
15	Title and credits	Title and credits
15	*Voice-Over.* "The learning process consists of training and education."	*Split-Screen.* Left: 3 year-old learning to read at the communicator. Right: Facilitator and group of 5-6 year-olds interacting around pictures of mammals.
15	*V.O.* "Training is the learning of skills to the point where reflexes are automatic."	*Full-Screen.* A pair of hands performing tasks automatically.
45	*V.O.* "Most training takes place during the first life-period. . ."	*Full-Screen, Series.* Children of 6 months to 6 years learning to walk—exercise—manipulate—use the communicator.
45	*V.O.* ". . .or the second life-period."	*Full-Screen, Series.* Children 7-13 years working at communicator—cooking—gardening.

Queries and Comments.	NO. OF SECONDS	AUDIO	VIDEO
	30	*V.O.* "A supportive social environment facilitates training."	*Full-Screen.* 3 year-olds being shown how to use the communicator by patient adults.
	15	*V.O.* "Most training is auto-learned by using the communicator."	*Full-Screen.* 3 year-old learning to read at the communicator.
	45	*V.O.* "All communicator training is programmed in INTER beginning at Level 1". *SPOKEN:* "Arms above your heads, now bend down, touch your toes."	*Full-Screen.* 3 year-olds exercising to communicator information.
	30	*V.O.* "Education is the experiencing and learning of problem/possibility areas."	*Full-Screen.* 11-13 year-olds being shown irrigation practices.
	30	*V.O.* "Education is at first with a facilitator."	*Full-Screen.* Sculptor helping 7 year-old boy to model.
	30	*V.O.* "Facilitators are competent in a problem/possibility area."	*Full-Screen Mosaic.* Facilitators working in a number of problem/possibility areas.
	60	*V.O.* "The verbal interaction between facilitators and those experiencing a problem/possibility area is in OUTER-INTER. Approximate questions are asked in OUTER, the facilitator converts this into INTER, then formulates a response in the low INTER level appropriate to his audience."	*Full-Screen.* Facilitator and group of 5-6 year-olds interacting around pictures of Australian mammals, including pictures of Koalas.

NO. OF SECONDS	AUDIO	VIDEO	*Queries and Comments.*
	SPOKEN. Child: "What's that funny brown animal with the little grey animal on its back?" Facilitator: "That's an Australian Native Bear, and that's a baby bear on its back."		
75	*V.O.* "As the individual matures, education increasingly takes place through group interaction.	*Full-Screen.* Group of 7-8 year-olds working cooperatively with construction sets. *Full-Screen.* Group of 14-18 year-olds interacting around building plans. *Full-Screen.* Group of Terran Interaction Facilitators interacting around the reconstruction of Calcutta in the Synergy Room of the Terran Communication Center.	
15	*V.O.* "The individual also learns through auto-education.	*Split-Screen.* *Left:* 7 year-old boy working with clay. *Right:* Same boy working with construction set.	
20	*V.O.* "Eventually self-learning is reached and the individual interacts with himself."	*Full-Screen, Series.* Adult heads.	

Queries and Comments.	NO. OF SECONDS	AUDIO	VIDEO
	45	*V.O.* "The individual develops an understanding of the patterns in his internal communication system."	*Full-Screen, Animation.* Internal mental communication patterns.
	45	*V.O.* "He becomes selective about information input and his communication patterns re-organize."	*Full-screen, Animation.* Mental communication patterns begin showing centers of convergence.
	20	*V.O.* "Finally he learns to control the rate of information input and his interaction patterns converge. . ."	*Full-Screen, Animation.* Convergence centers becoming perception flashes.
	5	*V.O.* ". . .and perception occurs."	*Full-Screen, Animation.* Single flash expands to cover the whole screen.

. . . . Lecture by D, Economist / Ecologist, during third rites-de-passage of Yvonne, his granddaughter and apprentice, with pre-comments by Teg *(Document 22)* **. . . . .**   *Queries and Comments.*

Late evening, May 17, 1994

Conditions. I've resolved the fear / fascination I have had with the possibility of underwater living since I first heard about its development. Strangely, I've never lived near the sea at all. And my visit here was an unexpected bonus because my choice of D for learning about economy / ecology was entirely due to Ben. It was only when I looked at the computer print-out on community conditions and clothing customs, that I realized I would be living under the sea.

I took the freight submarine from Calcutta to Marseilles because I wanted the experience of living under water before I arrived. The experience began straight-away in Calcutta because we boarded the submarine from the lower-level docking area. When the elevator reached minus 200 feet and we stepped out into the crowd already in the assembly chamber, the first people I saw were Juan and Mboya! They were standing with an unbelievably beautiful girl—blue-black hair, cafe-au-lait skin, green eyes—and they waved as soon as they saw me. They introduced the girl as Yvonne, the granddaughter and apprentice of D, the economist / ecologist. Apparently they had all been visiting the Multi-ecology Pisciculture center in Burma.

I felt that somehow Juan and Mboya looked smaller and seemed quieter than when I saw them at Owl Rock. At least, that's what I thought at the beginning of the journey. But by the end of the last evening, when we had a costume party, I began to think that their personalities hadn't changed. We were all supposed to come as Ecological Areas. I thought that I looked attractive as my own Quebec Dome-and-Environment; I was in white from feet to neck, had "fir trees" around my shoulders and a perforated clear bowl over my head. Yvonne, of course, came as an underwater ecological area; not very precise as to detail, but a fascinating combination of green and blue and silver.

Mboya's costume was a conical cape painted with the ecological areas of Mount Kilimanjaro. He was voted the prize for "information." Juan appeared with no costume at all and said that his nudity represented a desert area in the hottest season. Somebody objected that even the desert wasn't that bare of animal life. Yvonne pointed out that, as he was covered in hair, that represented too much plant life. The general opinion was that he'd been too lazy to think up a costume and that he wasn't contributing to the evening. An hour later Juan reappeared as "Maximal Timber Use." He'd shaved off patches of hair and covered some of the shaved areas with short green leaves to represent new growth, and others with long leaves to represent mature growth. Then he'd stuck chips of cork in among the hair in the unshaved areas to represent stumps and underbrush. He was voted a special prize for "Maximal Use of Self-Environment."

I've now been in Medaqua for two weeks and have spent almost all the time under the sea. The Mediterranean has returned to its earlier purity. I find I love the sea, but I'm experiencing daily living here as a series of tense situations.

The community residents are almost all uniquely interested in the evolution of underwater living and some of them are members of the Underwater Living P/P Institute. Many of them seem to me to feel quite unnecessarily threatened. I have heard an extraordinary number of conversations in which "they" (who live on land) have been blamed for the continuing slow pace of development of underwater living.

Within the community there is also sharp disagreement about the meaning and purpose of underwater living. The present community activity is sea-farming: fish are raised under maximal conditions in areas cut off from each other and the "open" sea by separation techniques I still don't understand. In addition, there is vegetable farming: some vegetables are very

similar to those grown on land and others have been evolved   *Queries and*
from sea-plants.   *Comments.*

Some of the longer-term residents have begun to question this community myth of sea-use, and are proposing a change to a myth of sea co-existence. They wish to convert to a vegetarian sea-diet and prevent the eating of fish. Given the fact that pisciculture is presently essential to protein adequacy throughout the scarcity-regions, the other residents think this is unrealistic. There are also a few residents who want to change over completely to a myth of sea-adaption. They propose surgical conversion of the human-being for water-breathing.

Medaqua seems to me to be an example of the danger of permitting a community to be dominated by the debates of a p/p Institute. The conventions and goals of the community cease to be accepted as a valid basis for life and there is constant tension. Indeed, if B was right in his description of the requirement for an effective SITUATIONAL—no unnecessary challenge to existing goals and conventions—communities with these conflicts are not functioning communities at all. Intra-community interaction is so weak that there is no reinforcement of the community myth and extra-community interaction by those in the p/p Institute continuously produces challenges and alternatives to the community myth.

D is apparently beginning to fear that the tension will force him to leave but he is consciously avoiding the issue. Anyway, this evening we're trying to put all this out of our minds. It's Yvonne's 28th birthday and she's celebrating her third rites-de-passage. It's perhaps the most important of all the rites-de-passage, for it marks the end of the period of preparation and the beginning of the period of full responsibility.

As part of Yvonne's celebration, she asked her grandfather to give a lecture in the grand style. D stood at a lectern used at the Sorbonne more than a century ago, which had been specially requested from historical-stores in Paris. The lectern had been placed so that the fish seemed to be swimming all around

D—a delightful incongruity. Yvonne invited her fellow apprentices and many of her peers.

Personal attitude. Entranced. The lecture slid by gently. I'd discussed this economic history with D before. He looked extremely handsome—if uncomfortable—in his "tails." The mood-creation was so successful that it helped to overcome the effect of Pill 2.

Text. Yvonne: I'm delighted you could all come this evening for my third rites-de-passage. As you can already see, this evening's celebration will start with something you have not experienced before. D is going to give a "lecture" in the style and manner he would have used in 1966, the year I was born.

He has asked that you keep several things in mind as he speaks. First, he gave his last lecture in 1975: this was the final time he was unable to insist on a more useful framework for interaction. Second, he will be speaking as an "economist" because economist/ecologists did not exist in 1966. There were then two main schools of economy: Neo-Keynsian economists who believed in the perennial necessity for economic growth, and classical economists who also wanted economic growth, but who believed that fiscal balance was ever more important. Third, D will talk as though he were in front of a North American audience because he spent most of his time there during the sixties. Fourth, he will give his lecture as if he were looking forward from the mid-sixties and forecasting future events.

D: Good evening, ladies and gentlemen. I have chosen to address you this evening on the subject of the change in economic thinking and economic trends, which I believe will take place over the next ten years. Predictions are, of course, dangerous, but it is necessary that we take risks occasionally if we are to get any view of the future.

My analysis starts from the assumption of John Maynard Keynes, the great British economist whose work has been adapted by the "growth" school. He stated that the condition in which his grandchildren (my children) will live must necessarily be profoundly different from those which existed in the 1930's, at the time he was writing. I fear that the predictions I shall make will seem unbelievable to many of you, for they suggest that conditions will change fundamentally before the end of the century. I am aware that this contradicts the views of most of those who are now coming to be called "Futurists": they normally seem to assume that, while there will be very significant increases in technical competence, socio-economic conditions will not be profoundly affected.

I could spend all my allotted twenty minutes stating the reasons why I am convinced that we must expect basic change in socio-economic conditions. Time pressure forces me to move on as rapidly as possible and I shall therefore begin my analysis with the views of the British physicist, Dennis Gabor:

> In today's world all curves are exponential. It is only in mathematics that curves grow to infinity. In the real world, they either saturate gently or they break down catastrophically. It is our duty as thinking men to strive toward a gentle saturation, although this poses new and very distasteful problems.

This insight of Gabor's has been confirmed by Irving Kaplan, an American consulting psychologist, who has stated that, given the accelerating rate of change, there are only three alternatives for the future:

> First, that the rate of progress in the technological world of the near future is beyond the comprehension of minds using the contemporary frame of reference. . . .second, a deceleration of technological progress, which could be due either to the exhaustion of technological potential or to the attainment of such a high level of technology that the culture would be saturated with the technological product and the society would shift its values. . . .the third alternative would be for the curve of progress to end or to fall precipitously. This could only indicate a catastrophic event such as a disease epidemic of tremendous proportions, a rain of meteorites, or a war of sufficient destructive force to destroy the nation's or the world's industry and technology.

*Queries and
Comments.*
I support Kaplan's view that we are limited to these three
alternatives. I believe that we can already perceive that neither
the first nor the third alternatives can be a possible route
into the future. I would hope that we all agree that we must
avoid the third alternative for it would destroy all the potentials we have so arduously built. The first must also be
avoided because it is clear that the human psyche cannot
keep up with the present rate of progress in the technological
world, let alone the rate inevitable in the future, if trends continue
to develop.

Societies will only perceive the need for a slowing-down of
technological change if their value systems have already
changed fundamentally. The arguments of the neo-Keyn-
sians, who assume that wants can never be satiated and that
continuous "growth" in production, achieved through increasing
productive efficiency, is therefore always valuable, can already be
shown to be ill-founded. Psychologists are now telling us that sensory overload is as damaging to the human psyche as privation.
People will therefore inevitably come to see consumption as a
means to the good life and not as the *good life itself*. The result
wiil be a consumers' revolt in the seventies; people will come to
limit their possessions to what they really need. The consumers'
revolt will be paralleled by changes in production techniques resulting from the cybernation revolution whose real implications
were stated so clearly in the 1964 document of the Ad Hoc Com-
mittee on the Triple Revolution. With the implementation of these
techniques, cybernated machine systems could take over large
parts of production.

But the effects of cybernation are still being masked today. There
is a continuing *decline* in unemployment rates at the present time.
However, this is due to four temporary effects: first, the Vietnam
war; second, the continuing extraordinary inefficiency with which
new computer techniques are being used; third, the willingness to
retain and hire people who are not truly necessary to the functioning of organizations. The fourth factor, which will become of
increasing importance, is associated with the third. More and
more people will prevent the effective functioning of machinery and
machine-systems in order to try to preserve their jobs. By the

beginning of the seventies, this movement will have grown to the point where it will be seen as a neo-Luddite revolt.

In the early seventies, there will be a general atmosphere of pressure tactics, disruption, and destruction. Neo-Luddite sabotage will reach epidemic proportions. It will take the form of direct destruction, the calling of strikes to prevent full utilization of equipment, etc. For a considerable period of years, the technological infrastructure of the society will function extremely inefficiently; in fact, there will be several periods when it will seem as though even minimal services cannot be maintained. (The beginnings of this development will be obvious in the big cities even before the end of the sixties: the productivity of the most creative members of the society will be drastically reduced as they try to obtain security and minimal comfort for themselves and their families.)

Neo-Keynsian economists will, of course, fail to understand the significance of these developments and will respond by attempting to keep the economy "growing" as rapidly as possible, thus overstraining the already malfunctioning infrastructure still further. They will point to their successes, however limited, in absorbing the unemployed as evidence that there is no need for real change. Their "growth" policies will prevent the bankruptcy of marketives and other organizations which no longer have real value to the socio-economy; these will continue to employ those types of people, and to use those resources, most needed elsewhere to strengthen the infrastructure.

Neo-Keynsian economists will fortunately be increasingly kept in check in the early seventies by conservative economists who are more concerned with "fiscal balance" than with "growth." By the mid-seventies, the neo-Keynsian preoccupation with "growth" will be modified by public concern over the resulting pollution and a growing understanding of the meaning of ecological systems. This latter development will result in particular, from the fact that we will understand that all production *necessarily* results in a larger amount of final waste and that growth in production systems must be accompanied by growth in recycling systems. In effect, the traditional economist's shorthand for the function of the economic system—PRODUCTION/DISTRIBUTION/CONSUMPTION—will have a fourth term added, RESOURCE RECONSTRUCTION. Thus, economists will become economist/ecologists.

The events of the late sixties and seventies which I have just described from the economist's point of view can also be summarized in socio-political terms: First, the continued, deliberate policy of overstraining both national economies and international exchange systems will cause growing instability with constant devaluations and an emerging trend toward protectionism in international trade policies and consequent international tensions. Second, public indignation at the attempt to preserve artificial scarcity by restrictive and disruptive practices in education, communication, transportation, construction, medicine, etc., will be reflected at the polls. Politicians will be forced to respond. Third, there will be a challenge to existing patterns of income distribution. This will start with complaints about the injustice of the relative tax load. However, as an understanding of the principle of artificial scarcity spreads, there will be governmental attempts to limit the wages, salaries, and incomes of those in the medical profession, the construction unions, and others who appear to the public to have taken unfair advantage of their power.

It also seems very possible that a fourth element may develop: legislation abolishing common stocks will be passed following the recognition that stock speculation is merely a *respectable* form of gambling.

In order to emerge from this multi-crisis, triggered by piecemeal governmental intervention, we shall have to change completely our understanding of the way the economic system works. We shall have to perceive that so long as the preservation of artificial scarcity is permitted, patterns of income distribution do not depend on the value of contributions to production but rather on the power each group has been given or has seized.

When we come to understand that, given the changes in the socio-economic system over the past half-century, the value of a person's contribution is not presently measured by his wages or salary, the first practical results will be the introduction of new forms of income distribution.

I foresee the need for two steps. The first is to provide everybody with a constitutionally-guaranteed, basic income regardless of the activity he engages in. It has been proposed that this should be called Basic Economic Security. I also see a transitional need to provide new forms of income maintenance for those who presently have higher levels of income, but who will inevitably lose their jobs to machines and machine-systems in the seventies; this proposal is usually called Committed Spending. This is necessary so that the individual can meet the financial obligations to which he is already committed. It is also necessary because the totality of these payments have been anticipated in long-term economic planning and a sudden cessation of payments would disturb national and even international economics.

Yvonne, ladies and gentlemen, I must end here, for my crystal ball would have seen no further. Indeed, I may already have shown more prescience than was available to me in 1966. Perhaps I should .remind you that you may "clap" at this point, if you want this speech to have the proper period flavor. I should add that even by 1966 I'd got rid of *that* particular pattern which aimed, in part, to permit the audience to feel that it had made its contribution and therefore had a "right" to forget what had been said and also to reassure the lecturer that his audience had not been totally asleep.

Certainly, none of D's audience had been asleep. When Yvonne announced a question period, explaining that this was the normal custom of the time, the only question was why didn't D continue, the lecture had been all too brief. D explained that in 1966 he wasn't anticipating beyond the mid-seventies, and

he felt his lecture should not do so either. He said that he'd
give us a very brief description of the events which actually
followed the introduction of Basic Economic Security and Committed Spending and then describe the roles which economist/
ecologists tried to fulfill at the present time, if we were really
interested, but that he'd have to continue from the point of
view of 1994. Everybody wanted to hear more, so D
continued.

D: New forms of income distribution did, in fact, develop during
the seventies. They were not what I had ideally hoped to see
because a constitutional guarantee of rights to Basic Economic
Security and Committed Spending was never passed. But the
degree of flexibility introduced into the socio-economy was sufficient to ensure two significant changes: one synergetic and the
other entropic.

The synergy occurred because, although most people still
performed their work as structured jobs in marketives, others
joined together in consentives in order to create a more supportive environment for their work (which was useful to the
society but which was not "profitable" for marketives.) At the
same time, a limited entropic change took place as consentives
were also founded by creative and imaginative people who
left key jobs in marketives and other organizations which
were without real value to the socio-economy. Their departure
destroyed the viability of many of these organizations. The
fact that these organizations had ceased to produce was not
detrimental to society, as some of their activities did not meet
any real needs, but their bankruptcy contributed to the socio-
economic and political collapse of the mid-seventies. This was
the time of the "entropic-seventies," of the Republican and Democratic realignments, of the creation of the Planning Party and
also the time when the ABC was putting its strongest pressure
on bureaucracies.

It was precisely those bureaucratically-structured organizations, which had been used to convince the population that they
should buy products that they did not need and should enjoy

situations which were actually intolerable, which collapsed. After their collapse, the reality of the seventies entropy became manifest to a growing part of the population. I personally believe that this factor played a larger role in the replacement of the concept of *anomie* by the concept of *amondie* than is generally agreed. People really became aware that their society was in breakdown, and that socio-economic and cultural confusion was worldwide. Nevertheless, the limited entropy of superfluous marketive and organization collapse was, of course, necessary and permitted the larger synergy of the seventies to take place.

I must add a parenthesis here. We are still not clear about the methods we can use to determine which local entropies are essential to larger synergies and which can be avoided without damaging larger synergies. This is probably the most critical theoretical issue confronting the Ecology/Economy P/P Institute at the present time.

By the beginning of the eighties, the economic situation was changing rapidly. The 1979 Scientists Synergy had reinforced concerns about limiting waste of materials and the time of creative people with vital skills and had also led to the end of the neo-Luddite revolt. The consumers' revolt of the seventies had helped people to perceive that the good life could not be achieved on the basis of an "ever-higher standard of living." The abolition of common stocks in 1980 made managers of marketives responsible to the society and not the stockholder.

Many personal and societal needs were being satisfied by the development of consentives. The goods and services produced by the consentives came to be known as sociofacts. As superfluous marketives had disappeared, those marketives which continued their activities were necessary to the socio-economy. Their level of activity was increasingly regulated by demand, according to "classical" economic principles. The goods and services produced by marketives came to be called ecofacts because they were sold on the open market with the price

Queries and Comments.

Queries and Comments. rising and falling according to the relation of demand to supply.

At the beginning of the eighties, economist / ecologists were acting as ecology facilitators. They were using a new shorthand to describe the systems with which they were concerned: RESOURCE CONSTRUCTION / PRODUCTION / USE. It was partly the clarity which resulted from this new analytical framework which helped us to understand that by 1985 eco-fact-production in North America was already fully sufficient to meet auto-estimated needs for ecofacts. Continuance of money as a rationing (or priority) mechanism was therefore no longer necessary. Today, as you know, North America, Australia, Japan, and almost all of Europe are abundance-regions and are committed to providing as many ecofacts to the scarcity-regions as can be absorbed without damage to their culture. This does not strain current productive potential in the abundance regions.

The main roles of the economist / ecologist in the abundance-regions presently are:

First, to ensure that auto-estimated personal needs for ecofacts and community ecofact needs throughout abundance-regions are available in the necessary quantities *without* forcing people into activities which they do not enjoy.

Second, to minimize use of materials which are in limited supply and which cannot presently be reconstructed by recycling or other measures. Despite the progress we've made in resource reconstruction and the very real possibility that a universal matter converter may be technically feasible, the interaction facilitators in the Ecology / Economy Institute agree that we have to be extremely prudent.

Third, to try to develop a conceptual framework within which we could create total, terran patterns of land use. Of course, even after we've established the framework,

we'll still have to deal with the reality that most communities are unwilling to cooperate in this area.

Scarcity-region economist/ecologists also strive toward the
goals I've just stated, but, in order to attain them fully, they
will have to create abundance. This requires, as in the abundance-regions in the past, that the amount of ecofacts available
be increased until it balances auto-estimated personal needs
and community needs. The task would be far easier if the
original definition of satisfaction in many scarcity-regions
had not been destroyed in post World-War II years. Most
non-Western countries traditionally perceived satisfaction in terms
of absolute amounts of consumption. This culturally-limited consumption pattern was destroyed in the postwar drive for economic
development, which was accompanied by the introduction of the
goal of maximum consumption.

Today the problem of increasing production in the scarcity-
regions is no longer a shortage of machinery and machine-
systems: abundance-regions have the techniques to produce
and provide fully-cybernated production marketives which
require little or no manpower. The difficulty is to introduce
these marketives into functioning cultures without disrupting
land-use or imposing distribution and consumption patterns.
During the fifties and sixties, economists undermined the
cultures of many scarcity-regions which were unfortunate
enough to be considered suitable recipients for aid. At least we've
learned enough to avoid *this* mistake.

So long as the division of the world into abundance- and
scarcity-regions persists, the threat of a total breakdown in
transnational understanding is possible. It is generally
agreed that abundance-regions bear the responsibility for the
continued existence of scarcity-regions. It is difficult for the
many in scarcity-regions who are poorly educated to comprehend why higher levels of ecofact transfer from the
abundance-regions to the scarcity-regions and higher levels
of emigration from the scarcity-regions to the abundance-

regions would be entropic. In fact, understanding of this point requires considerable sophistication in the use of system theory.

Thus high levels of tension are inevitable in scarcity-regions, particularly in non-functioning conglomerates such as Shanghai, Calcutta, Rio de Janeiro, and Lagos. In general, these tensions have so far been prevented from causing breakdown because there has been a rapid rise in ecofact availability throughout most of the scarcity-regions. It is only in the non-functioning conglomerates that socio-economic progress is not matching population pressure. I must add, however, that there is some evidence that the rate of improvement has not been as rapid recently.

I often wish that societies could have perceived the realities of the cybernation era a few years earlier than 1980. The scarcity-regions needed to move directly from the agricultural era to the cybernation era. By the time we had perceived this reality, it was already too late and most of the scarcity-regions have been forced to move through the cultural patterns associated with the industrial era before they can reach the cybernation era.

And now I intend to enjoy the remainder of the evening. What next Yvonne?

Yvonne: The dolphins want to do an aquatic display to celebrate with us. Can we have the room-lights out? They will start as soon as it's dark in here.

........**Extracts from first interview with E, Terran Interaction** *Queries and*
Facilitator with pre-comments by Teg *(Document 23)*........ *Comments.*

Late evening, June 6, 1994

Conditions. I flew practically round the world to get to Hawaii—
an experience I've never had before and one I certainly don't want
to have again. My sleep-cycle is still completely disrupted and I
feel out of phase with myself and those I meet. I suppose the whole
situation is made worse because I've been moving so long. I'm not
at all clear how I'm going to keep going till I'm due home in November.

Personal attitude. I made the mistake of over-anticipation. I've
always wanted to visit Hawaii because it is the site of the Terran Center. I've often thought that Teilhard de Chardin would be amazed if
he could come back and see how his concept of noosphere has been
realized in the Terran Center.

It was ridiculous to assume that Hawaii's special terran status
would be immediately obvious on my arrival on Oahu, but nevertheless I've discovered from my conversations that some of the population would like to abolish the special status of the island and have
the Terran Center transfer to Malta (which declared itself terran
territory last year). I think that the proposal to have the Center
transferred is only supported by a fringe movement, but it is
disquieting.

It's difficult not to cheat, consciously or unconsciously, about my
mental state at this time. I now see that I can really only be frank
about my personal attitude if I'm not experiencing information
overload. I'm confused.

I'm also exhausted—so exhausted that everything is affected. But I
am enjoying the fact that my facilitator here, E, is a woman. I believe she may provide one of the role models I'm seeking for my
personal life. She and her husband are both Terran Interaction
Facilitators here and work together. I'm disappointed that he's

away on an important facilitation trip this month and won't be back until July. E and her husband decided to have no children, but there are several in their community; as far as I can see, E is as much part of the lives of the children as are their own mothers and fathers.

Text. Teg: Before coming here, I'd somehow got the impression that all those in Hawaii had welcomed the idea of being a terran island with special status. I'm surprised at how many of the people I've met in the past four days are strongly opposed to the present situation.

E: You wouldn't be surprised by these people if you'd watched Hawaii's evolution over the past twenty-five years. In fact, any time I look back over those years—particularly if I re-read the newspaper editorials—I'm amazed that we've got as far as we have. As late as the end of the sixties, Hawaii was still trying to find its identity in emulating the socioeconomic development and cultural patterns of the American mainland. Because information transfer systems were so distortive in those days, Hawaii was in fact adopting trends and styles which had already been abandoned on the mainland. The concept that Hawaii might have an independent future serving as a bridge between East and West was not even being discussed.

Teg: How did the change come about?

E: It's always unrealistic, as you know, to ascribe a change in societal direction to any particular activity or event. I suppose, however, that as is so often the case, there was a limited entropic trend and a major synergetic trend. The entropy emerged from the fact that the immigration from the mainland was destroying the racial balance between Chinese, Japanese, and whites.

I believe the synergy came from the University of Hawaii. A small, but growing group of students and professors alerted the population to the consequences which could be expected if existing socioeconomic trends—particularly those on Oahu—continued till the end of the century. Subsequently, after several years of discussion, general agreement was reached about Hawaii's need to create a new future. By the mid-seventies, the university was already serving as the information center for Oahu and as a Pacific-area communications center.

Teg: Then Hawaii's Terran Communication Center developed out of the Pacific Communication Center? But I've heard that it was the increase in meetings and conferences around the potential of world organization which moved Hawaii into being concerned with world communications.

E: In the early seventies, more effective methods of information transfer began to be established among the many fragmented groups which were trying to move beyond nationalism. They became aware of the favorable conditions for transnational meetings which existed in Hawaii, and a growing number of world-oriented organizations therefore held their conferences and later established their headquarters here. From a terran point of view, as opposed to the traditional European and American point of view, Hawaii is central. Geneva seemed to be the geographical center of the world after World War I and New York the center after World War II. Once the world was perceived in terms of communication there was no longer a need for the concept of a geographical "center"; but the choice of Hawaii did serve to minimize total travel time.

Teg: Wasn't the whole development toward terran thinking threatened at one time by a lack of funds?

E: We were continuously underfinanced until the beginning of the eighties. It was only the funds forthcoming after the realization of the concept of world citizenship which kept us going. In 1975, 500 people, most of them liberal-humanists and some with international reputations, issued a statement on world citizenship. They announced that while they were not ready, for practical, and (in some cases, sentimental) reasons, to renouce their national citizenship, they intended to take up international citizenship as well. They appealed to others to join them.

The statement was not publicized. Each signer sent it to his immediate mailing list suggesting that they also sign if they wished to become world citizens. Many did sign and they also alerted others who they thought might be interested. One of the surprises of the process was how many groups, even in the same area, were unaware of the presence of others with similar views. Another sur surprise was that the news media took so long to become aware of what was happening. It was three months before the world citizenship initiative was noticed, and by this time, we could manage the difficulties created by the subsequent publicity.

Those who chose to become world citizens received the identifying symbol and were requested to contribute to the budget. The total budget was stated in an annual message to all world citizens and the percentage of income required in order to reach the budget was estimated on the basis of voluntary tax returns filed the previous year. There was no compulsion to contribute. It was found, however, that the minimum budget was largely met by world citizen contributions, and grants of various types prevented the financial situation from ever becoming non-viable.

Teg: What about the funds from the Scientists Synergy? B, the scientist I visited, told me that many scientists who considered themselves part of the Synergy and who agreed with the transfer of Synergy funds for terran activities contributed from one to five percent of their income.

E: Money from this source became available in the early eighties. Instead of being limited by a budget, large sums of money—at least by our standards—became available. We often felt it useless to spend our entire budget because we could not discover people with the qualifications to do the required facilitation, and when we did find them, they often didn't require funds for their support because they were already living on Committed Spending.

In fact, it was the *over*availability of funds which led to a crisis. Many world citizens were convinced that cooperation between large numbers of individuals toward common goals required formal organization into structures, using the Western pattern of parliamentary procedures. During the second half of the seventies, we had therefore concentrated much of our efforts on an attempt to create a world parliament to which each world citizen would elect

a representative. Some remarkably intelligent means were discovered to limit the divisiveness of the classical election process.
In particular, we planned to use the communicators, which were
increasingly becoming available for direct voter participation by
world citizens.

A world parliament during the seventies would, I believe, have
been very valuable. It would have provided a center from which
accurate information about present and future terran concerns could
have been disseminated. It could have developed a world constitu-
tion, which would certainly have been outdated by later events, but
which would have been a clear rallying point for those sharing terran views.

Throughout the second half of the seventies, we never had sufficient funding to bring such a world parliament into existence.
When funds did become plentifully available at the beginning of the
eighties, we had to decide whether the creation of a world parliament would still be constructive. Most of those still in favor of this
development seemed, from my point of view, to be arguing out of
ideology rather than in terms of the actual situation. They simply
postulated that a democracy was the best political system and that
Western-style parliamentary procedures were the only way to
achieve this democracy.

Those of us who had moved beyond the idea of Western-style
democracy argued several points. First, that elected representatives
do not formulate policy in response to existing situations but rather
in response to political conditions in their constituency. Second,
that the many p/p Institutes which had been created, partly under
our auspices and partly independently, were together fulfilling the
role of a world parliament. Third, ...

Teg: May I ask a question here? Many of those with whom I've
interacted this year seem to think that they and their colleagues
played the major part in the creation of the p/p Institutes. How did
they really develop?

E: I think everybody *did* contribute. This was perhaps the fundamental synergetic convergence of the seventies, which was masked
by the general entropy. To go back to the point I was making, the
third reason for moving beyond the idea of Western-style democracy
was that the patterns of behavior built into the Institutes seemed
far more likely to prevent people from abusing their position than
any technique one could structure into a world parliament.

Teg: Of course. Now I *really* see why I have to give A, the historian I visited, a zero for competence. If those related to the Invisible
College didn't fulfill their responsibility of accurately assessing
each other's competence there would no way of sanctioning incom-
petence or irresponsible behavior . . . . But surely the obsolescence
of the idea of a world parliament was already obvious by the
eighties?

E: Not really. In the early eighties we had only just begun to clarify the meaning of a communications society. Indeed, I myself still
felt uncomfortable arguing that there were more satisfactory forms
of government than parliaments and assemblies. It took us some
time to realize that parliamentary organization was fundamentally
bureaucratic and based on inflexible, irresponsible, structural
authority, and even more to understand that the type of organization required for setting up the Terran Center as a maximally functioning communication system had to be flexible and based on the
sapiential authority of responsibly-acting individuals.

We now know that our view was correct—but I don't have to remind
you that there were many liberal-humanists who left the terran
movement over this issue and who have not returned. Their 1982
breakaway over our plans for a Terran Center was a direct result
of their insistence on a parliamentary form of organization.

Teg: Well, I shouldn't complain. If it hadn't happened, there'd never
have been any Orwell Fellowships. It was, after all, the same group
of liberal-humanists who used their freed resources to create the
Orwell Foundation.

Perhaps this would be a good point at which to ask you about one
of A's historical interpretations because I'm beginning to perceive

that the shifts in alliances over the past twenty years were far more complex than I'd previously realized. During the seventies you were associated with large numbers of liberal-humanists while working with the University of Hawaii, on the Pacific Communication Center and toward world citizenship. Looking backward, how would you describe the roles of the ABCs and the liberal-humanists in the creation of the communications society?

E: Strangely, the liberal-humanists unwittingly achieved the goals of the ABCs. At the same time the ABCs' pressure tactics had, as their main effect, the prolongation of the industrial socioeconomy.

They involuntarily supported the goal of the liberal-humanists which was precisely to adapt and preserve the industrial system.

The worldview of the liberal-humanists who worked with us in the terran movement did not differ markedly from that of the liberal-humanists who were in power in the sixties and early seventies. They all believed that the industrial era could continue so long as modifications were made. As you discovered when talking to A, many of them have never understood, even up to now, the profound change required to move from the industrial-era to the communication-era. They still wish to organize the world along the same bureaucratic lines.

The ABCs, on the other hand, saw the need for fundamental change and the policies proclaimed as necessary by the ABCs were largely those which *were* required. It is ironic, therefore, that the ABCs were less effective in creating the communication society than the liberal-humanists. The decision of the ABCs to fight bureaucracies forced them to become like the bureaucracies they were fighting: conflict can only occur between those who essentially share the same view. In effect, the ABCs reinforced the industrial era. On the other hand, the evolutionary steps of the liberal-humanists, which they saw as perfecting the industrial-era, were actually the steps which led to fundamentally new situations.

Teg: In effect though, both the liberal-humanists and the ABCs were wasting most, or nearly all, of their effort because they did not understand either the world in which they were living nor the world they *would* be living in.

E: That's right. Neither group understood that we would have to develop a society in which the desires of the individual coincided with the needs of the society (the Benedict synergy-effect). They did not see that this would only be possible in a society in which the basic virtues of honesty, responsibility, humility, and love improved rather than damaged the position of the individual.

Nor did they ever come to understand that our communication society can only be viable if we learn how to avoid crises through effective information movement. Both groups continued to believe that pressure would always be required to bring about action because they thought that significant action would only be taken in crisis situations—a view that events over the past fifteen years have proved wrong both on the American mainland and here at the Terran Center.

Teg: I hope that I'll be able to spend a good deal of time up at the Terran Center while I'm here. As you may know, Hawaii is the only place where I've arranged to spend two months during the period of my Orwell Fellowship. I feel that it's essential to my future work that I understand the activities at the Center.

E: Yes. I've arranged for you to be at the Terran Communications Center during the next quarterly meeting, which is expected to last a week. I also hope that you'll be able to participate in one of the continuing games at the World Synergy Game Center. I expect you'll need to spend three weeks to a month there. In addition, I've arranged for a number of interviews with people who were active in the terran movement and who can therefore help you understand the past history and present developments of the Terran Center.

However, after seeing you today, I think we'd better put off any activities until you've had a rest. You don't seem to be in a fit condition to undertake such a heavy program of information intake.

Teg: I know I'm tired, but I think that once I've adapted to the situation at the Terran Center I shall be under less strain.

SECTION 111
SYNERGY –
MONTHS SEVEN
THROUGH ELEVEN

........**Record entry by Teg: Unanticipated return home to Quebec from Hawaii** *(Document 24)*...........................

Early morning, July 25, 1994

Conditions. My personal room in Quebec.

Personal attitude. During my time at Owl Rock, I discovered from Hassan and Luna that I had to learn the SITUATIONAL of each community I would be visiting if I was to interact successfully and, that to do this, I would need to gain a real understanding of the community and its behavior patterns. Reflecting on my residence in China, the south of France, and Hawaii, three communities where I really interacted, I think I learned this lesson.

But the last few weeks have taught me another lesson. In my attempt to learn so much in so little time, I reached a state of exhaustion through information overload. With too little time for mental reorganization of information patterns, my perceptions diminished and I finally became confused. I should have cancelled a couple of my interviews during the February to June period. It's entropic to change plans once they have been adopted, but I now know that it's even more entropic to go on with plans if it is certain that they will not work out.

I've seriously considered cancelling my September visit to G, in Artistia, but I think that I should go as I'll only be away from Quebec till the end of October. But now that I've seen the results of losing my capacity for reflection because of over-fatigue, I'm determined not to let it happen again. I really find it difficult to understand how people were able live in a permanent condition of mental and physical overstrain in the mid-twentieth century, but my parents assure me that they did.

Text. I'm just completing an unanticipated stay at home. I was so totally exhausted by the end of June that I had to leave Hawaii. I'm over my fatigue, and Pill 2, which I restarted yesterday, has not yet modified my enthusiasm. I was off the pill for a month during my time at home.

My medical facilitator in the community group asked me only one question about going back on the pill: "Do you want to?" When he heard my unintentionally dramatic "No," he recommended a further three months on the pill. He believes there is no need to worry when people don't want to use Pill 2—it was only if people became habituated to the emotional diminution associated with it that he discontinued its use.

I think my medical facilitator was mildly triumphant that his joking prediction during my final celebration before leaving Quebec in January had come true. He'd told me that I'd be under his professional care within half-a-year for overfatigue: I'd laughed at him. I suddenly remembered what he said on June 28 when I found myself unable to continue at the Terran Center in Hawaii.

I'd had a terrible night. For three weeks I'd been sleeping badly. As I never take any drugs that aren't necessary—this is probably why I'm so conscious of the impact and implications of Pill 2— I kept on refusing to take even the mildest form of soporific. After I'd finally got to sleep, the telins signalled and Shirley from Quebec said in her cheeriest voice that she just wanted to chat. I asked her if she didn't know what time it was in Hawaii (as if geographical area time had any influence on most people's internal time-clocks. I got the resulting confusion straightened out, but only several days later after I got back to Quebec.)

I then realized that it was my fault. I'd left my telins showing the wrong readiness state; its setting indicated "Willing to receive all calls." I didn't get back to sleep, of course, and next morning I almost omitted my exercises for the first time I can remember. I didn't—one of the few synergetic aspects I've got to remember about the end of my trip to Hawaii. But when I reached the part where I checked my "awareness" against my norms, I found the data really depressing. I arranged for an immediate computer-medical-record-compilation and I was informed that I needed to rest *now.*

Taking time out to rest seemed impossible. After all, one of the four annual general-meetings of the TCC was just about to be held, and I'd heard that it was probable that an emergency meeting would be called following some unexpected effects of recent climate-modification experiments. In addition, I was looking forward to accepting an invitation to participate in one of the Terran Synergy Games. (I'd met one of B's apprentices who'd come to Hawaii unexpectedly to work on the consequences of the possible extension of the lifespan by five years and he'd asked me to spend some time with them.)

Fortunately my interaction with E was synergetic so I immediately went to discuss the deterioration in my mental and physical state with her. As soon as I told her about my morning's awareness check she said I should follow the suggestion to rest *now*. She arranged everything and got me out to the airport for the next plane. She perceived quite correctly that I would only be able to rest in Quebec. Unfortunately, there was a confusion at the airport which we could not have anticipated.

The principle that planning always ensures spare capacity in transportation has been so long established that people have become careless about communicating their travel intentions. As intention to travel is under-reported, needs in transportation capacity are underestimated: just like any other ecofact, required transportation capacity is calculated according to information received about estimated needs, with only a very small surplus added. The only way that transportation can be available when required is, of course, for information to be passed to the travel center. But so many people are now failing to communicate their intention to travel that transportation capacity is now not always adequate to meet needs.

The demand for the flight which I was to take to the American Northeast was excessive as was that for several other flights leaving at much the same time. The consequent confusion was probably inevitable because most of those travelling had never experienced a similar situation; previously, they had arrived at the airport and proceeded straight on board.

The conditions were difficult but the airport facilitators should have been able to handle them since the boarding priorities are clear in these circumstances. All those who have communicated their travel

Queries and Comments.

intentions are boarded first: there will necessarily be room for them because, if the number of reservations had exceeded the capacity of the plane, a second one would have been available. Then any people who show Invisible College priority suffixes board. Of course, facilitators in the Invisible College only use their priority cards when their travel is essential. Those who have emergency reasons for travel then go on board, and finally the remainder in the order of their arrival at the terminal.

The airport facilitators seemed confused by the large crowd and unable to apply the priority rules. Two men in the fourth life-period eventually helped to allocate seats on the flight. I'd talked briefly to them and they said that I'd fall in the third category because of my medical emergency. I discovered before we took off that they had been participating in a Terran Synergy Game to discover the long-run results if failures to transfer information about travel intentions continued at this new high level.

The perpetuation of an abundance system depends, of course, on successful information systems. If it is not possible to estimate demand, scarcities inevitably emerge and some form of priority system is inevitable. However they are structured, priority systems within potential abundance-systems will inevitably lead to highly entropic situations. The two transportation facilitators told me that they had looked specifically at the implications of the fact that those associated with p/p Institutes are given suffixes which entitle them to priority in any scarcity situation. They had discovered that, although these suffixes are only used when essential, they will be increasingly resented by the public if transportation shortages should continue. The public is only aware of occasions on which the priority is used and not the many times that those with a right to priority do not take advantage of it.

As soon as we took off, I went to sleep. When I woke up at the end of the flight I felt even worse than when I boarded. I managed to thank the people who'd helped me and to get home somehow—I don't remember much. When I arrived, mother put me to bed. When I woke next it was seventy-two hours later. She told me that I'd had a three-day sleeping pill used to break a chronic case of fatigue. (My medical facilitator said nobody in the community had needed one in the last ten years.)

Two days later I joined up with a group of my peers up north. Since the recognition that pesticides must not be used except when absolutely necessary, some of the classic biters have come back in full force. I'm told that the mutations which followed the use of pesticides really increased itch levels. I believe that at the beginning of this century people went north in summer to hunt and fish. This July we were the game and the insects the hunters.

It's a lot less unpleasant than five years ago, however. The mosquito has been eliminated through the release of sterilized males, and a new technique holds promise for the elimination of blackfly. The process of controlling noxious insects has taken far longer than was expected when effective technologies were first discovered in the sixties. Implementation of elimination and control techniques was delayed by a growing understanding of ecological balance and concern about the possible effects of pesticides on total ecological areas. Full systemic analyses of the roles played by fauna and flora have turned out to be extremely slow, and it is only recently that the use of the available non-pesticide techniques for eliminating noxious insects has been resumed.

Of course, even if it seems fully clear that a species has no role in balancing the ecology of a given area, the species is not completely eliminated. Special areas are set aside for continuation of existing ecosystems, including noxious flora and fauna; these areas are left to evolve without interference, but are continuously observed. All-sense-tapes of these areas are available and they, together with all-sense-tapes of specific species, are the methods by which children experience those ecosystems they cannot directly observe. I went to zoos when I was young and did not understand, even then, how we could place animals in such entropic situations.

My talks with D showed me how much progress we've made in understanding ecologies now that ecological balance is no longer thoughtlessly destroyed for "economic" reasons. The conservation movements of the sixties often believed that there was a "natural" environment to be preserved, and absolute values attached to particular parts of it. Today our aim is to preserve all the species which the process of natural selection passed down to us, to create supportive environments for each community, and to ensure the continued viability of the terran gestalt.

........**First interview with F, Community Facilitator, with precomments by Teg** *(Document 25)* ....

Cool of the morning, August 3, 1994

Conditions. Emptiness. Again I'm struck by the fact that I sometimes feel expected sensations. Africa is still heavily underpopulated in many areas, particularly where I am, just south of Timbuktu.

There's been some immigration—and it's increasing—in an attempt to reduce population pressure elsewhere. It's only since the end of the eighties that there has been enough understanding between those promoting the idea of "negritude" and the northern peoples here that any significant levels of immigration from Asia or Europe have been conceivable.

The widespread intertribal conflicts of the seventies diminished rapidly in the eighties when it was recognized that the purely artificial boundaries created by Europeans around the turn of the century had no ultimate validity and that societal decentralization into communities was as necessary in Africa as in other world areas. Once the principle of societal decentralization was understood, the hostility between the formerly white-dominated south and the rest of the continent also began to diminish as South Africa was reorganized into viable communities.

Personal attitude. I'm very happy to see F again. I haven't seen her since we first met in Limoges, where she was looking into the possibility of ceramic arts for the community where she was then facilitating. Although I'm looking forward to working with F, I find that I'm no longer sure of exactly where I would like to start learning about community facilitation. Perhaps I'm confused by the amount and variety of information which I've already received from the communities I've visited this year.

Queries and Comments.

Text. Teg: Last year, when I was thinking about this month with you, I had a clear idea of what I was going to ask you. I had intended to find out about the seventies process of societal decentralization and how community myths got started. Now I find that I've got fragments of questions, rather than one definite topic to discuss.

F: It doesn't matter. You can just OUTER around them if you like. I'll get some idea of what's in your mind.

Teg: I've been thinking about Medaqua and the Najo Hills Research Community. Although one's in a desert area and the other's underwater, don't they really have the same experimental myth? And if so, why is Najo Hills functioning so well when the Medaqua residents are in constant conflict over the direction of their experiments?

F: But they don't both have the same myth. Because the Najo Hills consentives share the myth of experimental living, there are no conflicts over their general goals. On the other hand, the Medaqua myth is *not* experimental living, but underwater living. When those residents who are also members of the underwater p/p Institute propose continuous experimentation with the general goal of experiencing life under water, conflicts arise with other residents. Studies of societal decentralization have taught us that human beings can live according to a very wide variety of community myths, but that it is essential that the behavior patterns of the community accord with the community myth. It is when the real culture diverges too far from the stated culture that communities become entropic.

Teg: Do any communities have the same myth? During the first six months of this year, I've felt overstrained through trying to adapt to the myth of each community I've lived in. In three communities I managed to interact in the community SITUATIONAL; but by the end of June I found that I couldn't absorb any more. Isn't communication between communities becoming more and more difficult?

Queries and Comments. I've been wondering about this ever since I was at the TCC in Hawaii. E, the Terran Interaction Facilitator, told me that data were beginning to show rapid increases in the number of emergency meetings called by the Communication Centers of the Institutes to discuss the avoidance of crises. E said that she believed that this indicated an earlier communication and interaction failure and that the difficulty was the inter-community divergence between SITUATIONALS.

F: I *have* noticed a decrease in interaction between communities, but this is the first time that anyone has suggested to me that an increasing divergence in SITUATIONALs might be a contributing factor. We know that the SITUATIONAL communication style of each community reflects the community myth; we also know that as community myths evolve, and communication within the community becomes more synergetic, synergetic interaction *between* communities becomes more difficult. Perhaps I'd better do some thinking and data-gathering on this before we talk about the process of societal decentralization and the beginning of community myths.

........**Sixth interview with F, with pre-comments by Teg**
(Document 26)..

Midday, August 15, 1994

Conditions. Very hot.

Personal attitude. I've come to know F better than any other facilitator this year. Perhaps it's because this community is so small and isolated. She has convinced me, *intellectually*, that attempts to isolate a "woman's role" are meaningless. Given the fact that it's not possible to distinguish the contribution of those involved in any personal synergy, it is obviously *especially* ridiculous to try to separate out the potential of men and women, who, in most cases, need to interact with each other to discover their full synergetic potentials. (I'm not sure I'm going to find it easy to facilitate this insight for my mother. I *do* now see why the Friedan movement of the sixties to turn women into surrogate men and the reaction movement in the seventies to be "feminine" had to fail.)

Text. F: I think I'm now ready to discuss the question you raised during our first interview about the role of diverging SITU-ATIONALs in inter-community incomprehension. This question has led me to reexamine my presuppositions. The general theory behind community facilitation holds that communities can only be created by the discovery of a myth if individuals (and families) are already interacting in groups. If interacting groups do not form, communities cannot be created, however great the number of people. The total number of individuals and families remains a conglomerate—sometimes a conglomerate of millions.

I have been concentrating so completely on the facilitation of community myths *within* interacting groups, that until you raised your question I hadn't given much attention to the negative overall pattern emerging *between* communities. As soon as I started to examine these negative patterns, I perceived how important this might be. I've since put aside all except my top priority work to research the problem with my apprentices.

The emerging data indicate that the present pattern of social decentralization is now terranly entropic. There is also a possibility that it may no longer be synergetic even for individual communities.

The clearest way I can explain this problem for you, and perhaps further clarify it for myself, is to go back thirty years. The planning of the sixties had assumed that it was inevitable that cities of twenty millions, as well as vast megalopolitan areas, would be the pattern for population distribution by the year 2000. On the contrary, thirty years later, the present terran pattern in most parts of the world is localized communities, with the number of residents varying from five thousand to fifty thousand. (The only major exception to this pattern are the multi-million conglomerates such as Lagos.)

The extrapolations of the sixties proved incorrect because they failed to take account of a developing change in personal worldviews which was to reorganize living patterns. There was a growing concept that each individual had personal strengths which would be expressed in a unique personality structure, given favorable circumstances. The drawing of the inevitable corollary—that people can only find a suitable environment for their particular development if there are many diverse communities—became obvious in the early seventies.

I was living in the United States when the Planning Party, which had won the 1972 presidential elections, began to accept the concept of societal decentralization as a basis for policy, toward the end of their first term in office. It is rather generally believed that this is one of the factors which ensured their winning a second term.

The Planning Party decisions were immediately turned into action by those of us who had been discussing a theoretical decentralization of United States society. The basis for decentralization into communities already existed in the considerable range of sub-cultures which had survived the "American Melting Pot" cultural-assimilation process. In addition, some sub-cultures which had almost disappeared were revived, in changed forms, during the black and poor revolutions of the sixties.

As these country communities and these city enclaves and barrios began the process of self-development, the "community planner" of the fifties and sixties became the "community facilitator" who aided the community's self-definition process by using the new community-organization techniques.

As community facilitators passed from theory to action, they discovered that two steps were essential in community creation. First, it is necessary for those already living in an incipient community, or those interacting groups which want to form a community, to agree on the community myth and community goals. Second, there must also be agreement on certain basic behavior patterns: should people arrive on time? what is acceptable clothing? what days are the community celebrations? These arbitrary conventions serve to establish habit-choices.

The discovery of myths, goals, and behavior patterns for the communities in process of creation was complicated by the growing urban entropy of the seventies. The break-down of accepted forms of law and order, both in terms of willingness to obey the law and in terms of the ability to enforce it, made the cities so unsafe that many fled them. It was this entropic pattern, however, which opened up sufficient housing so that those in the worst slums could move into better housing and the slums were then demolished. The land thus freed was used to create barrier zones between increasingly autonomous communities. Though at first the zones were basically hostile, they later became neutral buffers.

Some urban communities in the city centers never developed a community myth; instead, they continued with the goal of maximum consumption of ecofacts. Some new communities were also founded by individuals committed to this pseudo-myth. As ecofact needs were held to be unlimited, and some individuals amassed huge amounts, these came to be known as Sensory Overload Communities.

These are not really functioning communities, and it is difficult for me to describe their behavior patterns to you. I think that life in a Sensory-Overload Community has to be experienced to be understood.

Teg: I'm going to Artistia for this reason.

F: Then you'll certainly find out what Sensory Overload Communities are like. These are "control" communities—controlled by the economic mechanism of pricing and differential income. As the goal of maximum consumption is economic, all decisions are subjected to economic mechanisms. Those of us now in the fourth life-period lived in societies almost completely controlled by economic mechanisms when we were young, so we essentially understand how these communities are organized. You will have difficulty, for you have never really experienced any other but communication communities with decisions reached through interaction in the community SITUATIONAL.

But this brings us back to your question. The basic functional mechanism of communication communities—decision-making through in-

Queries and Comments.

teraction in the community SITUATIONAL—implies a divergent
development of each community's SITUATIONAL and consequent
growing difficulty in communication between communities.

Teg: One of the people I visited this year, an historian, argued that
divergence between communities could be prevented if each community contained residents from other communities. Do you think this
is true?

F: Obviously not. Only those who share community goals and behavior patterns can be involved in the process of future-creation
within that community. Those from other communities cannot share
community goals without becoming part of that community. It *is*
true, on the other hand, that all communities should share terran
goals. According to the data we've been examining this week, there
has recently been a slowing down of terran synergy, not only because of the increasing divergence in SITUATIONALs, but also because of changes in work patterns. When present communities were
first created, the people in them were so proud of making their own
decisions that they were willing to fulfill all the service sociofact
needs of their community—fire-fighting, health facilitation, and so on.
Indeed, they were also very willing to respond when neighboring
communities needed aid. Today, however, communities are increasingly unwilling to help others when difficulties arise.

Looking at the data, I realize we should have perceived this change
in work patterns and community views before. I believe that we
were blinded to them by the apparently successful transnational
synergy of the last ten years. In the mid-seventies, the degree of tension between the abundance-regions and the scarcity-regions was so
great that it appeared that the scarcity-regions might be preparing
to use all their available weaponry—including bacteriological, chemical and radiological—against the abundance-regions. But by the mid-
eighties, levels of tension were declining following the increased transfer of ecofacts and technical assistance to the scarcity-regions.

Unfortunately, the continuing transfer of ecofacts, machines, and
machine-systems is increasingly seen by many in the scarcity-regions
as requiring no contributory effort. Inhabitants of the abundance-

regions have also come to believe that the availability of ecofacts will continue even if decisions are not taken or communicated. Individuals and communities are not even always communicating the required information to ensure that their ecofact needs can be met.

There is therefore a tendency for the rate of increase in ecofact availability to decline. If this trend should continue, the scarcity-regions will not succeed in abolishing community credit-cards by year 2010 as had been planned, and the abundance-regions might even be forced back to scarcity patterns and distribution entirely on the basis of a priority system.

If our continuing research over the next few weeks confirms the existence of these entropic developments, I shall need to change the direction of my work. I have, of course, a responsibility to try to convince as many people as possible that present patterns of terran societal decentralization are now entropic, but I fear that most of those who should be concerned will not "hear" me. At 60, I'm much too young to waste the rest of my life persuading my fellow-members of the Community Facilitation p/p Institute that our patterns of analysis and action no longer respond to developments in intra-community and inter-community situations.

It seems to me that you're beginning to define a new direction for your own research. Perhaps you can tell me briefly at this time what your present ideas are, and then you can let me know later in the year about your final decisions.

Teg: Following the interviews I've already had this year, I believe I'm beginning to perceive three elements in a new phase of terran synergy. First, there is the serious, but potentially limitable, entropy which is emerging as communities cease to be able to inter-communicate, as those in them cease to work effectively, and as they come to believe that ecofact availability can be ensured without decision-making and communication of necessary information. Second, as those individuals in the second and third life-periods perceive this entropy, they are becoming aware of the need for a world-wide terran myth which will be incorporated in the SITUATIONALs of all communities. They do not want to abandon the diversity created over the past twenty-five years, but they do wish to place it in an overall framework. Third, mankind has begun to look forward to the year 2000 as a significant year, although nobody seems yet to perceive how it will be significant. I had thought before I started out that plans for renewed terran synergy around the year 2000 were more advanced than they presently are.

........Tel from Hassan to Teg re convergence of thinking *(Document 27)*...

10:17, September 3, 1994

Text. You must have begun to think that nobody at the Orwell Foundation was reading any of the material you have been communicating; computer records show we've sent you nothing except a health wish in July. DON'T WORRY: we've been supportive of all those who most needed it. In particular I know you'll be glad to hear that Olaf is having a highly productive year and that Mitzy will also benefit, although she's needed a personal facilitator for most of the time. By the way, we learned a lot about your personality as well as Juan's and Mboya's by comparing your accounts of the time on the submarine between Calcutta and Marseilles.

You can expect to hear from us more frequently from now on. Our reorganization difficulties at Orwell are over. The Board of Directors have formally relinquished their structural authority and have agreed that all those who are interested, including the past Fellowship holders, should make decisions on policy in group interaction. I think about two-third of the Board will continue to work with us, and some of them have already begun to recognize how much harder they'll have to work from now on.

This tel also comes to let you know that there seems to be a convergence between your thinking, as expressed at the end of your August 15 interview with F, and ours. We agree that there is a largely unperceived terran crisis. We believe that the Orwell Founda-tion may be able to contribute knowledge and skills to the crisis resolution.

Queries and Comments.

........**Letter from Teg to peers in Quebec re Teg's first nights in Artistia** *(Document 28)*..

Dear peers,

Midnight, September 5, 1994

Conditions. Room in hostellerie. (Read on.)

Personal attitude. I'm not sure.

Text. I'm not sure of anything except that the following tale of my misadventures will amuse you, or shock you—I don't know which. We've always been taught about the dangers of sensory over-load but I didn't know what they meant until I got here. When I first wrote to G to ask if I could visit him I received a charming reply, but since then there's been no response to my communications, so I decided to go to the community guest house. When I requested the address from the communicator, the print-out stated that there was no community guest house but that the function of lodging those without hosts in the community was carried on by hotels. As I wasn't sure of the meaning of the word, I asked for a definition and received: "Hotel./ ho-tel/ n. Marketive providing all services to visitors for money. Obsolete concept in all areas where money has been abolished. Usually replaced by community guest house."

I teled D in Medaqua for information on the reason why money was still being used in Artistia. He informed me that money served two purposes. First, it gives an artificial value to products which would otherwise be considered worthless. If Artistia's products were distributed as sociofacts, people would not accept them. The founders of the community, and most of its residents, have never experienced any distribution system except priced products and limited income.

It doesn't seem strange to them that a number of ecofacts, many of them worthless, should be arranged in a value-hierarchy according to the price. On the contrary, this hierarchy is an essential part of their way of living; because each individual's products have a value, the individual sees himself as having a greater or lesser value (but at least some value), a role, a reason for living. It is because the people in Artistia are not self-validating that they need validating by the pricing of their products.

Second, as Artistia is not a communication society, goods are provided by the economic mechanism—which thus controls the society, even in the absence of a bureaucracy. There is no real community-myth in Artistia and therefore no socio-cultural basis for establishing community goals. Without a community myth, overall community synergy is not possible and some form of social class system is inevitable. In Artistia individuals are ranked according to the monetary "value" of their product: this also serves as an allocation mechanism to deal with the reality of ecofact scarcity. Although Artistia and the other sensory-overload communities are in abundance-regions, a scarcity situation is inevitable within these communities because there is no auto-estimation of ecofact needs; estimation of needs is replaced by distribution of ecofacts according to ranking in the price-value hierarchy.

The monetary mechanism is used for distribution. The higher the ranking, the more money an individual has. This, in turn, insures a greater ability to obtain ecofacts. The accumulation of ecofacts is a public demonstration of ranking in the price-value hierarchy: wants are therefore unlimited. The overconsumption, or rather accumulation, by those high in the value hierarchy, reduces the amount of ecofacts available to meet the real needs of those low in the hierarchy, and an ecofact scarcity therefore exists.

Finally D reminded me that I need not worry about money because I had, of course, a terran credit card. I wasn't really worrying about that aspect; my concern developed as I looked at the characteristics listed by the hotels. The "best" boasted that they had the full range of equipment for sensory excitation both in the public and private rooms, including the provision of "any desired partner human or mechanical." The minimum admitted to by any hotel was "modern and every provision for sensory stimulation." I chose that hotel and had to move immediately because I discovered that the only reason they made no provision for finding sexual partners was that it was assumed that anyone staying there would naturally be willing to participate with everyone else. I ended up staying at the "poshest" hostellerie in town; at least it has locks on the door.

I assumed that all this was simply the exploitative face of Artistia and that as soon as I could reach G everything would settle down. Reaching him was proving unexpectedly difficult. I had already discovered before I arrived that he was never available by telins and my communicator print-outs hadn't received any response. Finally, earlier this afternoon, he teled. He sounded bored, but when he heard my voice he seemed to become interested. I must have been stupid but I *still* didn't understand. I read some of the most pornographic literature of the early seventies just after my second rites-de-passage—my parents felt it would deter me from those patterns of sexual behavior and it did—but my experience up to now had led me to believe that everybody found them quite as ridiculous as I did.

G invited me round for interaction late that evening. This is entirely a night city; people get up as the sun goes down and go to bed with the dawn. The pattern's exhausting for me because I'm a morning person—only the fact that the soundproofing has to be perfect in order to permit the sensory-excitation machines to function permits me to get a night's sleep at all. Earlier I had startled the night clerk when I asked for the sensory equipment to be turned off. He told me it wasn't possible. But I'd already discovered that everything could be bought here for money and so I got what I wanted by showing my terran credit card.

G's apartment (which he described as his "pad") contained all the latest equipment. At least he assured me of this when I arrived and, given the range of effects which developed during the hour I stayed, I can well believe it. I know, of course, that feelies described by Huxley in *Brave New World* had turned out to be not

Queries and Comments.

only possible but were now considered technically primitive; but I still didn't know what that meant.

I found myself with several feelings warring in me. First, all my intellect revolted against the sensory overload being forced on me. Second, it was clear that those who were designing the sensory excitation techniques had discovered ways to directly affect certain centers of the brain. (I'm convinced that if I'd not been on Pill 2 they'd have overwhelmed me.) Third, I think I was slightly influenced by the still sometimes-heard argument that one cannot decide on the value of something without experiencing it.

But my strongest reaction was that G and his pad were ridiculous. Although he kept watching me intently and moving around in a personal-approach way, his very ridiculousness prevented me from being as worried about myself as I should perhaps have been.

Three or four times I laughed just when I obviously shouldn't have. When I saw how upset this made him, I was worried. This year I have really learned not to ridicule other communities' behavior patterns.

Eventually I left. Fortunately Artistians rely on their machine-effects for coercion: physical force is never used here. Since I returned to the hostellerie, I've been watching one of the frothy, early-thirties comedies. When it's finished, I'm going to try relaxing with the Marx Brothers—ridiculous love scenes and all—and thinking back to the many times we've seen them together.

It's strange, one of the things that has kept me going since I arrived in Artistia, was a tel from Hassan informing me that my thinking is moving in the same direction as those working on the reorganization of the Orwell Foundation.

So, Forward,

Teg

........**Letter from Teg to Ben re events in Artistia** *(Document 29)*

Early morning, September 7, 1994

Personal attitude. You may wonder why I'm sending this to you when it would be printed-out by your communicator anyway. But I think I detect your synergetic hand in the events of the past few hours, particularly as you were against my coming here in the first place; and when I did insist on coming you wanted me to see some-one else other than G.

It's all right. I'm not angry with you. I suspect that I would have been if you'd acted this way earlier in the year, but I'm now better able to know when I need help. This time I certainly did. I don't even feel very angry with myself. I'm beginning to perceive that fail-ures are inevitable when one is attempting to synergize; the critical necessity is to learn from failures rather than to permit an entropic pattern to develop following them.

Anna (see below) and I are going to tour Latin America for the rest of the month. I'm looking forward to being on a pleasure boat again; I have happy memories of crossing the Atlantic with some of my peers just after my second rites-de-passage. Of course, with the Atlantic crossing, we knew we were going months beforehand, so we were able to participate in the voyage celebration planning. My group did an "advertising" night. A group is going to do one this time so Anna and I will help with that.

By the way, I didn't tell Anna about my suspicions of your role, for I thought it might embarrass her.

Text. I got up early yesterday afternoon when the streets were deserted and walked around trying to get an impression of Artistia. It's fantastic. They have *real* advertising and hucksters. Every space is filled by a marketive trying to get you to spend your money and each assaults the senses more than the last—even when customers are not around. Eventually I found a place which was relatively quiet and which had just opened. Its sensory pattern was that of a left-bank Parisian cafe in the existentialist fifties; it must have been one of the least noisy in Artistia.

Somehow, I'm still not clear how it happened, but I found myself comfortably in conversation with Anna. It wasn't the fact that she was a girl because I was aware that sexual attraction here is not limited to members of the other sex. I suppose it was largely the fact that she wasn't in a high-dress—the first person I'd seen wearing an ordinary recyclable dress since my arrival.

Anna and I talked all evening. We stayed in the cafe for awhile; it provided us with a vantage point to look at the high-styles. We wondered why neither the men nor the women seemed to have any idea of how absurd they looked. She tells me that nobody here exercises or diets so that they are physically degenerating by the time they're thirty.

By the time that Anna and I agreed that there was nothing really amusing in the passing scene, I had already suspected that she didn't belong here. Later when I visited her home, I knew it. Her cottage looks over a stretch of Caribbean beach and is outside the limits of Artistia; she has to use sound-screens to keep the noise out so that she can enjoy the sea-sounds.

She told me briefly what she was doing here, but she wasn't inclined to be overcommunicative so I didn't press her. Anna and her colleagues live here in order to inform young people who drift into Artistia of the other options open to them. I gathered that nobody playing this role stays for more than a year and nobody is in the city for more than two months out of three.

The real artists are, as I had already realized, not here at all. The products of Artistia bear no relationship to the kind of work I saw at Picture Rock. The "artists" here do not interrelate with nonartistic residents, nor do they interpret or illuminate any community myth. There is no demand for or acceptance of Artistia's products outside the community.

The work done by Anna and her colleagues in the community is known and tolerated because they make no effort to change the life of Artistia, only to provide information about other options. Indeed, there is a significant minority in the community who know they're trapped here and, although they are unable to break away themselves, want to prevent others from wasting their lives.

In effect, the style of life known in Artistia and other similar communities reinforces personality weaknesses and rapidly unfits people for living in any other communities. The avoidance of decision-making by living as "free individuals," the concentration on immediate sensory satisfaction, and the immediate elimination of any form of uneasiness makes it impossible for people to go back and accept a pattern of life where tolerance of delayed gratification and uncertainty is necessary and where responsible decisions about goals must be made with others in the community.

Perhaps the most extraordinary aspect of Artistia is that it would not survive without continuous in-migration. Practically all of the women choose to be sterilized soon after their arrival for they do not wish to have to "modify their artistic self-expression to raise children." Practically the only people who leave Artistia, after they've settled in, are those women who have decided they want to raise children.

Anna told me more about the export-import situation. She said that while there are limits to the amount of ecofacts that the abundance-regions would supply to Artistia and other similar communities, Artistia did receive considerable amounts of imports. Their exports are negligible because Artistia products do not find acceptance outside the community. The abundance-regions consider that the provision of goods is of very little importance compared to the psycho-social gain from isolating these people with profoundly entropic

Queries and Comments. personal communication patterns, particularly when they congregate together of their own free will.

Although the grouping of individuals into communities such as Artistia is voluntary, these communities correspond in function to the prisons and psychiatric hospitals of the industrial era. They remove from society those who are unwilling to behave according to accepted behavior patterns and are unable to discuss community goals.

Artistia and the other communities were founded during the societal decentralization of the seventies by groups of people from abundance-regions who had never found a goal for their own lives and were therefore unable to visualize a synergetic myth for a community. The communities they founded have pseudo-myths including the spurious validation of the individual through "pricing" his work.

Most of the residents in, and permanent immigrants into, these communities are now into their fourth life-period and no communities of this type have been founded for the past ten years. It is now believed that advances in understanding of the learning process have ensured that those now in the first three life-periods are self-validating and that they will never need to found spuriously validating communities of this type.

........Letter from Ben to Teg in response to Teg's letter
(Document 30)...

Late morning, September 7, 1994

Conditions. The dome is open. It's a beautiful morning. Since I started raising the issue of claustrophobia there's a growing, willingness to consider whether we've been making really flexible use of the dome.

Personal attitude. Relieved. I felt that you'd reached the point where you understood the need for help as long as it was given only when required. I still play the old Beatle's classic with its line "I'll get by with a little help from my friends."

Text. But I didn't suggest to Anna that she take you off to Latin America. Do you have any objection if I join you? If you don't, tel me where and when.

I need to look at the Latin American situation. I now fear, partly as a result of your community facilitator's data, that it's not going to get out of the community credit-card system until people are once again willing to do more work. If this is true, my former estimates of developments over the next fifteen years are certainly wrong.

........**Main points of first interview with H, Information Processor, with pre-comments by Teg** *(Document 31)* ....

Morning, October 9, 1994

Conditions. Spring. Both in South America, where I was for most of September, and now in the eastern highland of Australia, new life is emerging everywhere.

I now know that I'm not going to continue to live in Quebec. This is partly an intellectual decision to facilitate the work I'm going to do. (Note to myself: that way of putting it made me realize that I was approaching the decision-making stages about my course of action over the next years.) The work will not be possible if I haven't moved away from where I grew up. Changes in attitudes between people still almost always require a period of absence.

In addition, I now know that I want to live in a different environment. I like snow, but I really do dislike being cut off from the outside for so long during the cold season. The increase in engineering and architectural capabilities has opened up whole new regions of the world for habitation. One of the unexpected developments of the past fifteen years has been an increase in the range of community living patterns: the rush to the tropics so obvious in the sixties and seventies ceased at the beginning of the eighties.

Personal attitude. I want to use my time here with H to get his help in creating synergetic personal information patterns.

Text. H: You're coming to the end of your Orwell Year. You weren't able to give me much idea of what you wanted to know when you first asked me for an interview. Perhaps it's clearer now.

Teg: My main information need is a personal one. I'd like to learn how to avoid information overload. I'll have seen facilitators in eight p/p areas by the end of the year, and knowledge about continuing research in seven of the eight seems essential to what I'll be doing in coming years; but obviously I cannot keep up with all of them.

H: Avoiding information overload depends partly on developing an appropriate attitude to communication and partly on screening out unwanted material. We're still struggling to discover the full meaning of both of these statements because it was not until the late seventies that the necessity of avoiding information overload was recognized.

Teg: The negative effects of information and sensory overload began to be recognized at much the same time then?

H: Yes. But in the sixties the difficulties were already obvious. In fact, a new definition of an optimist and a pessimist became current at that time. It was based on the fact that everybody involved with ideas necessarily received more paper than he could possibly read. The papers, articles, brochures, pamphlets and so on were therefore piled on every flat surface in the room until the piles became psychologically threatening. The pessimist then simply took all the piles and threw them out. The optimist went through the piles, putting aside the material he was *absolutely* going to read: this became the foundation for the first *new* pile.

*Queries and
Comments.*

By the early eighties, the piles of paper bought or given to the individual or sent through the mail were being replaced by a pre-selected information system. This system followed the creation of the p/p Institutes in the early eighties, and their many convergent predecessors in the seventies. These laid the theoretical groundwork for pre-selection through the structuring of information print-outs over communicators.

Today each person has to make his own decisions regarding information intake as he moves from the apprentice relationship to take up his full responsibilities. He determines what information he "must" receive. He then pre-selects by setting his communicator to print-out the messages he has decided he wants.

There are three major categories of information materials: The first category contains materials from the p/p Institutes. The Communication Center of each Institute has two major responsibilities. First there is the continuous updating of a statement describing ongoing research in each area. This statement is divided into:

the *dialogue-focuser* which outlines existing agreements in the p/p area and the clearly defined disagreements.

the *dialogic debate* which states the reasons for the disagreements; disagreements recognized as now almost always resulting from different conceptual frameworks.

the *psychebank* which suggests in mosaic form elements of a comprehensive structure which could encompass the different conceptual frameworks.

As you know, each Institute puts out its statement in video, audio, and written modes at levels from one to ten. Each Communication Center is also responsible for compiling a summary of events of relevance to those working in the p/p area.

Category 2 consists of a daily summary of terran events compiled by the Terran Communication Center. This, like the summary of events compiled for each p/p area, is usually very brief and general because people today are interested in trends rather than events.

Category 3 consists of the work of the Participant Communication Services which are responsible for evaluating new materials and operate independently of the Institutes. We still have difficulties in defining the concept of significant new materials. We *do* know that the most critical aspect is the occurrence of an explicitly or implicitly posed new question. However, what are the criteria for evaluating whether any question would open significant research areas or would lead to the discovery of new information about existing p/p areas?

You wanted to know how you should avoid information overload. As your work will require that you be aware of developments in many p/p areas, and also of new research, I would suggest that your most effective method of operation will be to program your communicator to receive: *Category 1* Significance 10 (the most important) modifications in the statements of all Communication Centers, as well as events in each p/p area at Significance 10; *Category 2* information on terran events at Significance 10; *Category 3* material from the services responsible for evaluating new materials at Significance 5.

These programmations will ensure that you do not customarily receive more than an average of 10,000 words a day, and much of this print-out you will be able to discard without detailed examination. Of course, it is also possible that a print-out would provide further research leads which would mean requesting other materials. In this case your print-out total for the day would greatly exceed 10,000 words.

I hope that this has answered your question about personal information selection. Are you also concerned about the general subject of communication?

Teg: Yes, that's been an increasing worry for me this year. At first, I tried to interact in my own SITUATIONAL when visiting other communities; later, I overloaded my mental integration processes by interacting in the SITUATIONAL of each community. I'm wondering if there's any solution to such difficulties. Is anybody working on terran SITUATIONAL?

Queries and Comments.

H: No. The only real present effort is to improve communication by manipulating the sense environment in which people interact in order to create cooperative moods. It doesn't appear to me that this is likely to lead to more effective communication.

Teg: Since you made that point, I'll ask you a question. I and a number of my peers have a feeling that most of those in the first two life-periods and some of those in the third are developing their reaction to sensory input to the point where present technical and artistic manipulation of interaction environments will be ineffective and even dangerous for them: the overload phenomenon again.

Because they *have* undergone full development of their senses, it seems to me that they might find a way out of the present difficulties resulting from the use of diverse SITUATIONALs in inter-community interactions. In effect, their understanding seems to be based on those micro-communicators which are still often seen by those in the fourth life-period as "over-sensitivity" and extra-sensory perception.

I'm concerned about the possibility of groups learning to communicate in this way because of two factors. First, the experience in the early seventies shows that people can easily destroy themselves if they become fascinated by mysticism. Could the same pattern occur following the development of micro-communicators? Second, how are entropic consequences to be avoided for those in the fourth life-period who probably can no longer develop their micro-communicators? There's some evidence that those in the third life-period can do so, but I think that the education patterns of the forties, fifties, and sixties were particularly damaging to communication-sensitivity.

H: There's an answer to the first question, but I know no fully

satisfactory one to the second. Those of us who were caught up in
the mysticism of the seventies were interested in such gross phenomena as telekinesis, telepathy, and, to some extent, thought control.
Capacities of this type are very unevenly distributed in human groups
and therefore the inevitable scarcity patterns developed. Those who
had these capacities wanted to use them for self-aggrandizement;
they were interested in drawing followers to themselves, rather
than using their capacities to benefit those around them.

The best research evidence now available suggests that micro-communicators exist in all human beings, but that they cannot be used

unless they are developed through sense stimulation. Given the fact
that these capacities are abundant and not scarce, the results of
developing these potentials, while certainly not completely forsee-
able, will certainly be very different from the results of the mysticism of the seventies.

The second question you raise amounts, in effect, to a continuation
of the "Moses" situation. Moses was permitted to see the promised
land, but he could never enter it. Beginning in the early eighties,
we have already been through one generation whose cultural attitudes
were such that only a very few could enjoy the world that was
coming into existence. We discovered that people were willing,
when necessary, to sacrifice their most cherished beliefs and to
see their familiar environment destroyed in order to ensure the
continued evolution of mankind. If micro-communicators should
come into use, probably another generation would have to go through
the same experience.

Before we break off, let me ask you if you'd be willing to let me
nominate an individual for a 1996 Orwell Fellowship. I believe that
one of my apprentices, Rama, would make the most of the opportunity.

Teg: I can't give you an answer now. I'm still puzzling about the
most appropriate way to choose the nominator of one of the 1996
Fellows.

........**Conversation between Teg and Ben re Teg's learning during year, with pre-comments by Teg** *(Document 32)*_____

Queries and Comments.

Mid-morning, November 15, 1994

Conditions. Home in Quebec. We've been having an unusual late fall. Beautiful days, although the mornings and the evenings have been cold. I've been taking full advantage of the weather because Ben suggested I did not come in to discuss my future plans with him until I'd not only got my thinking clear, but also my emotions balanced after coming off Pill 2. Of course, I've seen Ben and talked to him casually, as well as to my whole family and immediate community. I found some of them to be slightly annoyed because I'd gone north in July and really not seen them at all, but we're over the consequent difficulties.

Personal attitude. I'm off Pill 2. It's a wonderful feeling. But I didn't make a mistake, I needed the pill both to get me through the year and so that I could learn how to interact at a lower emotional level. I'm still emotional—and always will be—but I'm no longer emotional about my emotions. I can analyze them and begin to perceive which patterns I must create to employ my emotions functionally instead of letting them be a weakness.

It's just as well that I have achieved a better balance for I can see that my decision to leave here will be hard to implement. In addition, a lot of people are going to try to convince me that my future plans are unrealizable for somebody still in the third life-period. But I've had time to think about my plans and I've decided that I am ready to move from preparation to responsibility. Now I can benefit from a conversation with Ben.

Text. Ben: I've been rereading your year's communications over the past few days. It seems to me that your original plans and expectations were considerably changed over the year, particularly during the second half. If so, what do you intend to do now?

Teg: My expectations *did* change over the year. When I started I believed that:

Queries and
Comments.

First, terran society was moving steadily through the transition from the industrial era to the new era of information 'communication 'cybernation.

Second, the year 2000 was being seen as a focal point for terran development, in particular for terran synergy.

I now know that my expectations were over-optimistic. I believe the reason I reached them was that I had been receiving biased information because of the SITUATIONAL here at home. Our Quebec community has already understood the philosophic basis for the new era and incorporated terran synergy into community goals. Because our SITUATIONAL manifests this change in goals, I was assuming that the drive to terran synergy was common to all communities. As soon as I began to use the SITUATIONAL of other communities, I realized that several understandings were absent or inadequately expressed. Many communities still do not fully understand that:

Every individual is unique: the form which his uniqueness takes will be affected by his genetic inheritance by by his socialization process, and by his environment.

Real change can only take place through process: change must be evolutionary in appearance if it is to have any chance of being revolutionary in its effects.

Processes of change, both for the individual and the society, conform to synergetic and entropic spirals. The ways in which synergetic spirals can be continued and entropic spirals can be reversed are known in theory, but are very often difficult to apply.

The human values of honesty, responsibility, humility, and love are essential if synergetic spirals are to be predominant, if the Benedict synergy-effect is to occur. Effective communication depends on these values.

It appears to be primarily this fourth understanding whose significance has not been fully comprehended in communities around the world. It is true that most people recognize that their *own* community interaction is only successful when based on these values, but they have not generally perceived that inter-community inter-action must also be based on them. Nor have they perceived that each individual is a member of the terran society, and needs to be involved in terran communication as well as effective communication within his community, immediate group, and family.

Communities appear to have moved only half-way into the new era. At the end of the industrial era in the sixties, societies in abundance-regions had developed cultures which had replaced human values with the industrial-system necessities of dishonesty, irresponsibility, pride, and hatred. But human-group survival required that industrial-era necessities be rejected. This occurred, but only *within* communities. There is now a growing dislike of other communities, accompanied by a denigration of other community cultures, a distrust of them, and a denial of obligation to aid them. All of this has led to a diminution in inter-community interaction.

The infrastructure which is required to maintain a system of terran societal decentralization demands understanding, communication, and decision-making. The willingness to communicate and to take responsibility is declining and with it the capacity to create and preserve an abundance of ecofacts. In addition, many communities are becoming unwilling to produce the sociofacts required for re-inforcement of community goals and realization of community myths.

Following my Orwell Year, I am convinced of the existence of critical entropies. My question now is whether it is possible to avert a terran crisis. My feeling is that there is now insufficient time to avert a crisis because the entropic trends have been perceived too late. Do you feel the same way? You have a longer view of developments because you were involved at the beginning of the societal decentralization process.

Ben: I'm not sure that I really know how to answer your question. Should we compare 1994 with the time in the fifties, before the sixties confusion, when intelligent decision-making would have limited the entropic events of the seventies which followed the ending of the industrial-era? Or should we compare 1994 with the seventies when the fifties failures in decision-making had ensured that major entropies were inevitable?

What has changed since the last time in the fifties when decisions could have limited entropies? And where have advances been made over the last thirty-five years?

We have reached both an understanding of, and a high level of practice in, ecological balance. Population growth has almost ceased and intelligent human migration patterns are beginning to decrease population pressure on resources where it is presently most severe. We reversed the trend toward air and water pollution in the early eighties and have abolished the use of broad-gauge pesticides. We are beginning to perceive how to conceptualize plans for total terran land use.

We have also learned that neither physical nor mental coercion is an effective way of securing change: bureaucracies, legal systems based on precedent, money, riots, jails, schools, universities and mental hospitals no longer function as control-systems in abundance-regions, and are rapidly being changed in scarcity-regions—except, of course, in the conglomerates.

We have replaced these control-systems with communication systems. We believed that as patterns of environmental destruction and human violence had been eliminated, communication mechanisms would ensure both intercommunity interaction and community decision-making and that decisions would create resources.

If people continue to interact for synergetic decision-making, crises are averted; however a failure to make decisions permits crises to develop. Once there is a crisis situation, all decisions will inevitably be made by a few individuals who assume structural authority roles: a control system thus re-emerges and replaces the communication system. Lack of communication leads to scarcities and the management of scarcities requires control-systems.

We have recently been moving toward limited crisis situations

through lack of decision-making. Possibly this is because most com- *Queries and*
munities, and certainly practically all of the abundance-region *Comments.*
communities, have large numbers of residents who are in the fourth
life-period and therefore went through their learning process at
a time when self-control was dominated by exterior coercion.

These entropic trends could, if continued, reverse the eighties-
synergy. They were, however, probably inevitable given the assump-
tion-patterns of most of those in the fourth life-period who continued
to believe throughout the seventies (and, in many cases, right into
the eighties), that economic and social techniques would solve
human problems.

We did successfully create an ecofact production system based on
cybernation, an inter- and intra-communications system largely
based on new information techniques, and a terran community
system based on decentralization. It is now clear, however, that
far too little thought was given during the eighties to the concomitant reinforcing of the human personality and human behavior patterns. At the present time, ecofact abundance is becoming insecure
because people are too "lazy" to communicate their needs, residents
of communities are beginning to re-experience anomie, sociofact
production is diminishing because community myths are no longer
completely supportive, and ethnocentricism is reappearing because
the divergence between community myths is accompanied by a
breakdown in inter-community interaction as SITUATIONALs grow
further and further apart.

I *do,* however, perceive one aspect of the situation which leads
me to believe that we still have time to avert an overall crisis of
the magnitude of the seventies. In 1994, even if we are not attaining
our goals, we at least have a greater general understanding of
where we want to go, and what our goals are.

I think that the main block to goal attainment is our continuing reliance on societal decentralization as the terran myth. At first this
stimulated a richness in human thought and action which was terranly
synergetic, but recently this myth has become divisive and terranly entropic. We need to create a myth of joint terran synergy, not

simply of separate community synergies adding up, by some form of "Adam-Smith-invisible-hand" mechanism to terran synergy. If I've understood you, this is the area you want to work in?

Teg: My present plan is to bring together a group of terran-oriented people to interact on the creation of a joint terran synergy myth. Decision about activities cannot precede the formation of this group, but my present assumption is that we need to create a minimal vocabulary/for introduction into the SITUATIONAL of each community, which will facilitate discussion of the common myth. I'm also assuming that the year 2000 will be the most appropriate time to introduce the joint terran synergy myth. Perhaps the most synergetic way would be to introduce a terran calendar starting with Terran One to replace the year 2000. The Terran Celebrations marked by the calendar would emphasize the contributions of all regions.

Ben: Are you ready yet to discuss your way of bringing together the comprehensive group you'll work with?

Teg: Not yet. I want to get a small group together to discuss this. Will you join us?

Ben: Yes, with pleasure.

SECTION IV
DECISIONS - LAST MONTH

.......Letter from Ben to Teg re future plans *(Document 33)..*

Midday, December 1, 1994

Conditions. Computer-ideal again. But I'm old enough to appreciate the comfort of the dome in winter and now that we open it, when appropriate, in the spring and fall, I won't be leaving.

You'll gather from that statement that I'm not coming with you to help you create the new Institute. (Don't use that word — Institute — for you're going to create new patterns—and new patterns should be signalled with new descriptors.) It's not that I don't want to come, but I've seen too many people prevented from moving out of their apprentice relationships by the best-meaning facilitators. I don't think that I'm the type to fall into this trap but . . .

I'm willing to work with you, of course.

Personal attitude. The joy-sadness which comes when synergy leads to fundamental change.

Text. Here's the letter I wrote you at the beginning of the year:

Early morning, January 1, 1994

Dear Teg,

I'd have been delighted to nominate you for an Orwell Fellowship at any time, for you are undoubtedly the most dynamic of all the apprentices I've ever had. At this point, however, I'm hoping that what you learn will not only help *your* life development but, will also have considerable significance in changing the direction of Invisible College thinking.

Before the beginning of the information era, there were three theories about the degree of human freedom. One of them stated that man has no freedom: he is caught in a web of circumstances from which he can never escape and which cannot be changed in any significant way. The second theory stated that every event, however miniscule, changes the future of the world. The third theory stated that there are always a few people who have both the imagination to understand the trends of their time and and the courage to try to affect them in the direction in which they feel they should go. This last theory has always been my assessment of the degree of human freedom up to the end of the industrial era.

A basic goal of the communications era is to eliminate the pattern where only a restricted number of people are able to bring about change. In order to do this, it is necessary that information perception, communication, and decision-making be widely diffused. So long as crises can be averted, this goal is realistic. If, however, we fail to perceive entropic patterns until they have developed so far that a crisis can no longer be averted, we are necessarily driven back to the industrial-era pattern in which a few people have the major responsibility for situation-control.

I have recently observed some emerging behavior patterns in which control appears to be replacing communication. I believe that we can no longer simply assume that the functioning of terran society in the new communications era will necessarily continue to move away from entropic patterns. I'm now beginning to re-analyze the functioning of terran society.

It is my hope that the information you obtain may contribute to this re-analysis.

I really don't need to add much to my January 1 letter. You've done more than I expected, even more than I hoped for, during the last year. Now, you've set yourself a task which will require all your imagination and courage.

You told me Luna celebrated her third rites-de-passage when she was twenty-four because she had decided what she wanted to do; I've also heard of other people doing this. If you wish, I'd like to work with your parents on creating an early celebration of your third rites-de-passage. We could tie it in with the beginning-of-year celebrations. We could also use your idea of celebrating new developments over the last year—I'll celebrate the spring and fall opening of the dome.

Ben

........Tel from Teg to H, Information Processor re right to nominate Orwell Fellow for 1996 *(Document 34)*................

11:27, December 15, 1994

Text. I have today informed the Orwell Foundation that I have selected you to nominate a Fellow for the year 1996. As you know, this nomination is not subject to any form of review, so perhaps you'll want to tell Rama so that he can start thinking about what he wants to do.

I had some difficulties with this decision, but finally decided on the basis of two factors. First, I like your choice of Rama; having talked to him I feel he will benefit from the Fellowship year. Second, you're the only person who asked me for the right to nominate. As all facilitators are aware how Orwell Fellows are nominated, this suggested to me that they didn't have anybody who they felt would benefit particularly.

........Teg's Auto-Bio: Short Form *(Document 35)*............

Prepared: December 1994

Born Arizona, 1974, August 3

Queries and   Rites-de-Passage: 1st life-period to second: Quebec
Comments.   Rites-de-Passage: 2nd life-period to third: Quebec
                  Rites-de-Passage: 3rd life-period to fourth: Quebec (January 1, 1995)

Major strengths: Good cross-cultural communication skills
                    Ability in gestalt creation

Languages.   Excellent English
                  Excellent French
                  Excellent Chinese
                  Excellent Spanish
                  Some Portuguese

Communication Styles. Practice in OUTER, particularly
                          OUTER-INTER conversations

                          SITUATIONAL, learned in Quebec
                          City, but with wide experience of
                          adaption to other communities

Travel. Multi-community

Major life-events. I moved from Arizona to Quebec at the age of five. This left me with a tendency to emotional excesses which I have now learned to balance, having completed a period on Pill 2.

My socialization took place in Quebec. I was primarily introduced to the assumptions and activities of the Invisible College, particularly those in biology/ecology. However, the community is balanced, and I gained experience in many other skills and interests.

My apprenticeship was with a synergist in Quebec. During my apprenticeship with him I became concerned about possible entropic implications of the societal decentralization of the seventies and the eighties. He nominated me for a 1994 Orwell Fellowship which enabled me to explore the area.

I am just now completing my Orwell year. I am now convinced of the existence of critical terran entropies.

Area of interest. Creation of joint terran synergy myth. (Unavailable as facilitator unless directly concerned with work outlined above.)

Life-plan for beginning of fourth life-period. It is my intention to create a comprehensive interaction group to define the nature of the present entropies and determine the appropriate action-patterns for producing a joint terran synergy myth. The interaction group will have a preponderance of people in the third life-period, but there will be several people in the fourth life-period.

I anticipate that this area of interest will be time-limited. It seems to me that the reversal of present entropies must be sought in the "Terran Rites-de-Passage" between the second and third millenia.

........**Tel from Teg to Hassan re closing of Teg's Orwell Fellowship record** *(Document 36)* ....

10:00, December 23, 1994

Text. This final tel will close the records for my Orwell Year. All the material is stored under the appropriate computer codes and I have also made a summary selection for those who wish to get a sense of my learning experience during the year. The last document is my Auto-Bio, prepared December 1994. It shows that my intention is to create a comprehensive interaction group to define the nature of the present entropies and determine the appropriate action to create a joint terran synergy myth.

I am aware that the Foundation actively discourages major decisions immediately after the Fellowship year ends. I clearly perceive the reasons for this policy, but believe that they are not applicable in my case.

Given my decision, your recent tel informing me that there seems to be convergence between the thinking of those at the Foundation and my own, and the fact that all those who are interested in the Foundation now make policy in group interaction, I wish to formally request a meeting to discuss our convergent concerns.

I believe that the interaction should be mainly face-to-face and will require five to seven days. I'd find it easiest to go to Najo Hills. I believe that the Communications Consentive at Owl Rock would offer a maximizing environment for our purposes.

........Tel from Teg to all contacts during Orwell Year *(Document 37)*...

9:29, December 23, 1994

Text. This tel comes to thank all of you for your part in my successful personal synergy in 1994. I've chosen one frame of each of you from the 4 millimeter camera record, which typifies you for me, and am transmitting it with this tel. I'm also sending each of you the frame of me which I believe typifies me for you. Choosing these pictures helped me to perceive not only how differently I must appear to each of you (in many cases I'm wearing a high-dress loaned by the community store) but how much I see myself as having changed during the year.

I don't expect you to keep these pictures, of course; memory-books were an industrial-era pattern. But I did think that they would help you to see my view of you. This is important because I owe each of you the right to decide whether you want to be associated with my future plans, which you all have, in your own ways, helped me to define.

I'm transmitting herewith the text of a brief November 15 conversation with Ben, my synergist recommender. This summarizes the development of my thought during 1994 and the initial direction I'm planning, as well as Ben's reactions. A selection of the material I've compiled during the year is now computer-stored.

I plan to begin work toward creation of a joint terran synergy myth with a general introduction meeting early in 1995. If you would like to be present, or would like to participate over video, please tel me as soon as you have had time to review my materials.

. . . . **Tel from Hassan to All Participant Communication Services** *(Document 38)*. . . . .

13:57, December 27, 1994

Text. We recommend that you consider for potential distribution the material transmitted herewith. This is the report of "Teg" about her learning experience during her Orwell Year of 1994. She has already made a selection of the material compiled and we are in general agreement with it.

The finding of the report is that critical terran entropies are now developing, indicating a possible reversal of the eighties synergy.

READERS' RESPONSES

Queries and
Comments. This printed version of *Teg's 1994* is the second edition. The book
was first distributed in mimeographed form in 1969. We felt that a
mimeographed edition would best serve our aims: a) distribution
to the limited numbers of people then interested in the interrelation-
ships between ecology / systems / a human future; and b) stimulating
reader response around these shared interests.

Each mimeographed copy distributed contained the following invitation:

> *Teg's 1994* is a participation book. The information and
> ideas on which it is based come from many individuals. We
> hope that this process will continue, even though the book is
> now 'printed.' We do not consider that the act of mechan-
> ically inking these words on paper has given the contents or
> the organization any final form.
>
> You are, therefore, invited to participate in this focus on
> the future and you will find that space has been provided for
> this purpose. We suggest that you work in three stages: 1)
> Read through and note your queries and comments. 2) Read
> straight through your own notes, answering your queries
> from information elsewhere in the book wherever possible.
> You will probably find that your own notes are basically a
> summary of your views. You may also gain new perceptions
> of your own attitudes, as in a Rorschach test. 3) Send a sum-
> mary of your notes [to us]. . .

We do not anticipate that any reader will find his ideal future society mirrored in this book because this is not a Utopian description. *Teg's 1994* sketches a possible future world where the techno-system acts merely as infrastructure, expansion and growth are no longer goals, and human society has re-emphasized social interaction through worldwide decentralization into small, sub-cultural communities. But the process of change is continuing, and we are witnesses to it through sharing Teg's thought and experiences throughout her year of travel of 1994.

Queries and Comments.

During her year of travel as an Orwell Fellow, Teg learns that her contemporaries' concept of the 'communication society' is increasingly flawed by interaction failures between diverging societies. A full expression of each community's sub-culture, or myth, has been achieved only at the cost of increasing mutual incomprehension, and even a re-emergence of an aggressive community ethno-centrism. In the last decade of the twentieth century, there is a growing awareness that maximizing social interaction is as much an avoidance of the individual's responsibility for full self-development as were earlier a reliance on the control-systems of the 'economic mechanism' and later the 'technological imperative.' As the book ends, we see Teg and her contemporaries beginning the struggle for full human awareness through reappraisal of communication techniques and a new understanding of the role of the individual as a member, not only of a face-to-face community, but also of the larger human society—terran society.

A great deal of the response came to us not in writing but in face-to-face conversations or over the phone. The statements below are printed in chronological order of their receipt; they span the period January 1970 to April 1971.

We have edited these responses when the comments were so elliptical that they could not be followed without constant reference to the text of *Teg's 1994,* and/or in order to stay within reasonable length limitations.

Queries and
Comments.

Permission has been granted to reprint the material published here. Where writers have agreed, we have also printed their names and addresses. This will make it possible for those who wish to participate in the exchange of ideas around *Teg's 1994* to correspond with those who have already commented on the book.

Some people have written in INTER, some in OUTER, and some in SITUATIONAL—indeed at least one person writes in two different styles in his two responses. Whatever the communication style used, the responses are exuberant with the sound of people thinking.

1

Being a housewife responsible for budgeting and maintenance of the objects necessary to our present life style, I find the idea of obtaining ecofacts without any economic transaction a great idea. The current Master Charge plan seems a step in that direction. However, how do you envision effective distribution of needed goods? Eliminating the tedium and wasted time engendered by the care of clothing by use of recyclable and instant-clean clothing seems great. We must definitely spend more time working on the more significant matters which concern us individually and the world in general. Full use of men *and* women in their intellectual capacities is most necessary.

The political struggle between the ABCs and the Planners seems most plausible in view of the current situation. The downfall of the ABCs is most definitely rooted in their inability to provide a suitable alternative to what they are aiming to destroy. Their inability to think beyond removal of the current bureaucratic system is their Achilles' heel. Of course, the Planners would succeed in view of the fact that their "plan" makes economic sense to a business-oriented society. Thank heavens for the Scientists Synergy in 1979. It seems to hold forth the hope that the world will not succumb to the disaster of complete chaos. It seems as if worldwide decentralization even with the flaws which Teg encounters in her year of travel is a step in the direction of a saner world than the one we currently are faced with in 1970. I believe the difficulties can be eliminated. It would be a relief to know that effective world-wide birth control will become a reality and that the techno-system will no longer dominate our complete existence.

The whole lecture by D., Economist-Ecologist, during the Third Rites-de-Passage of Yvonne, his granddaughter and apprentice, was fascinating. Adding Resource Reconstruction to the economic cycle of production/distribution/consumption seems most intelligent and necessary. Why wasn't it incorporated sooner? The deceleration of technological progress and the view of consumption as a *means* to the good life and not as the good life itself seems most needed and sane. Maybe if we worry less about who has what and how much, we can concentrate on making the world a better place in which to live.

The problems encountered in the small, subcultural communities will yield to solutions. The change you have envisioned is not ideal in all respects, but it is a plausible and livable situation. The main problem seems to be to avoid entropic situations. Entropies are what originally caused the turmoil of the sixties but Teg shows foresight in planning a meeting toward the creation of a joint synergy myth to prevent a repetition of entropic situations. There seems to be hope for the human race....I will reread *Teg's 1994* again several more times this year and will let you know if I see things differently.

— —*Arlene Crandall*
7405 North Hoyne
Chicago, Illinois

2

I have been a little bothered by Teg. This, I now realize is because it is a form of teaching and programming, despite the fact that it solicits interaction. The essence of my argument is that if man is to develop his potential he must learn to learn. Teaching deprives him of the opportunity to do this. The whole concept of teaching is authoritarian and, I suspect, society's method of maintaining con-

stancy via control of the mind. The pre-school years of a child's
life are when he learns the mostest the fastest. He is learning to
learn when we tell him to stop learning and start being passive so
that he can be stuffed with the filling provided by school boards, state
dept's of Ed., the U.S. Office of Ed., and various contributing propa-
gandists. My own research and observations have convinced me that
the human seeks learning actively. One must only make the materials
available. Thus, I don't like a teaching strategy. Even one such as
in Teg. I wish for the era when all strategies are obsolete.

— —*Irving Kaplan*

3

I've reread parts of Teg and found new things I wasn't aware of
the first time around. Hope your prediction about effective birth control is not set back by the negative aspects being brought out by
the Senate subcommittee investigation.

——*Arlene Crandall
7405 N. Hoyne
Chicago, Illinois 60645*

4

Section 1. While certain NEW information is being communicated,
it seems that the subject of 'environment' becomes the aesthetic
justification for doing so, and as a consequence the structure dominates the style. The remainder is free of this consideration and
reads, for my part, much more freely.

Although sex does not seem important as part of the discussion,
certainly the Energy available in a guilt-free society would become
very important in determining and discovering the NEW myth
which will be able to command a common allegiance. For example, the desire and need to communicate...to another or other
forms of life in the Universe, the very Act, realizable or not, becomes a PROCESS worthy of aesthetic as well as practical consideration and the subject matter of our NEW myths.

Question: Has the concept behind words like RORSCHACH and
GESTALT been preempted by INSTANT communication in the elec-
tronic environment!?!

The image of MAN as opposed to the image of men, both psychologically and physically (color), is certainly bound to undergo
greater changes, due to genetic interference, much before 1994, yet
this does not seem to enter in as a consideration in the discussions
of "cultural divergence.

*Queries and
Comments.*

> ——*Lian O'Gallagher*
> *36 Waverly Place*
> *Chinatown, San Francisco*
> *California*

5

I'm reading Teg with much interest and with some perception of
the world you envision. I see it as more continuous with the present and take heart that there are some salutary arousals to danger
occurring. How effective they'll prove to be, I can't guess. More of
this later, however. Part of the hope is such changes as your work
(our little book, too) push forward. I see that there is opposition
gathering against the present Nixon-pushed guaranteed income
plan, yet Nixon's housing man proposed, last month, for the first
time in America the very usual continental abolition of the difference between rent and mortgage payment, a move to return the inner city to its inhabitants by letting them buy their own places once
again, a sure way of stopping the abandonment of inner-city rental
housing. Then there's mobile housing, a new solution of the needs
for further dispersal and for new housing of the urban-fringe people. Wherever I drive (Florida, Va., Cal., etc.), we still abandon the
institutions of the past (railroads, housing trades, inner city) without replacement, simply by letting them wither away; but we do,
without knowing it, invent new ones. Being no economist, I can't
judge the scale or the effect of such developments.

6

It is necessarily hard to appraise what this manuscript says, for
the end of Teg's Orwell year is her beginning, and presumably
ours. Thus, that which is forever in first draft, as I understand this
manuscript to be, doesn't allow for final criticism. Perhaps, though,
some first draft criticism can be permitted, relative to what the book
intends. And what the book intends, I believe, is good, as ambig-
uous as it sometimes is.

Queries and Comments.

Evidently, some approach like to the Scientist's Synergy plan will be eventually necessary to save us from the "entropic" cycle in which the world finds itself. And it is pleasant, if not foolishly optimistic, to think that scientists would initiate such an approach; for I suppose the ultimate power rests with them, the present unacknowledged legislators of the world (more on this later). The later development of, for instance, Orwell Fellows, who become members of an invisible college where conceptual thinking is pursued, rather than simple reactive thinking, is promising as well. As an instructor, certainly, I find that the inability to think conceptually is one of the greatest deterrents to acquisition of knowledge and creative thought. But, conceptual thinking is surely as old as Romanticism. But, the consequence of conceptual thinking is a problem/possibility attitude toward our dilemma which places its ultimate solution in the hands of the terran, or the people, not in the hands of power. I am not sure how this is to be accomplished, but this is a participating book, and thus my doubt participates. Communication is a key to people-rule (or participation), and the ultimate relocation of people in communities of manageable size contributes to solution. But, as the manuscript says, when community goals or myths are established, they come into conflict with the myths of other communities. An approach to solution of this problem is the establishment of a world-wide myth, to which various communities pay a kind of federated allegiance. OK, notes toward harmony and peace.

Authority in the world of 1994, it is to be noted, rests in communication centers, not in industrial-war areas which heretofore have produced chaos, for their leaders have naturally been more in sympathy with dishonesty, irresponsibility, pride, and hatred than their antonyms. It is difficult for the reader of 1970 to think of authority in centers of communication and information rather than in centers of power. Doesn't authority, to us, mean power? Here it means power to create benevolence by communicating with each person, if possible, to remind him of his individual power, his privileges— and his responsibilities. Thus, as the script wisely says, a recognition of the constant possibility (and apparent need) of change is vital to the world community and its awareness of responsibility. Authority in the long-haul becomes sapiential authority among the people: the wisdom to know and to think. It effects a synergetic attitude toward life and man's salvation. But since in the beginning sapiential authority seems to be the province of the Orwell Fellows among the invisible college, one is reminded enough of Plato's philosopher-kings to think doubtfully. But one has to begin somewhere, and this book does in hope.

Queries and Comments.

But unfortunately, the society outlined reminds me of a kind that Orwell might create, but to which he wouldn't subscribe. It sounds as sterile as the political, or economist/ecologist, language which describes it. The reader is made aware of communities by name, and their location is generally geographically fixed. But frequently these communities have domes over them for elemental control, and their purlieus are brought to our attention only in vague references, apparently to indicate that they are there, that this is a real conditional world, *c.* 1994.

The lack of concrete references is disturbing. A defender of the script would of course say that this is not the point, that this is the outline of a world which ought to exist and that detailed reference is irrelevant and unrealistic. Granted, maybe. But the rational process which conceived this world is the same one which gives us only rarely a comment on items to which the senses respond: we hear of sea sounds and Ben (Teg's instructor) speaks of "the joy-sadness which comes when synergy leads to fundamental change." Earlier we learn that Teg dislikes onions, but this is an emotional response which apparently is to be corrected. This she does, in part, by swallowing Pill 2, which lowers her emotional responses enough to allow her intellect a grander operation—so that it can understand properly the SITUATIONAL in which she finds herself. As a matter of fact we are frequently reminded that Teg is sensitive, emotional; and in respect to her and us we are told (besides the confusion resulting from information overload) of the entropic effects of sensory overload. I must, then, admit that I can't identify with these people. I can't see them as human, and so they bore me.

But it follows that I'm not supposed to see them as people. I'm supposed to see rather the synergetic, conceptual attempts to come at the problem/possibility factors in the world. That is, the objective economist/ecologist presenting an obvious problem with possibilities of solution. The rest is to be filled in. I would fill it in by making it validly an existential or Gestalt condition (of which the script makes mention). I would make it more human.

I refer to emotion, of course, to the spirit. Sex, not surprisingly, has little to do with this script, for "emotional clues" are to be subordinate to conceptual thought. Where sex is given some heading is in the community of Artistia. Artistia is a holdover community from the sixties, where money is still used and categorizes the worth of a man, and the population is consumption-oriented without shame. Sensory overload is the consequence, as it is the consequence of the society we live in today. Here Teg, a precocious girl of twenty, speaks of, and rejects, pornography. Pornography, it is implied, is concomitant with sensory overload. I doubt it. Perhaps the Victorian period gives evidence that this is not so. There sex was forced underground, but arose elsewhere in surprising and varied abundance. I imagine pornography (admittedly a seller's market at present) is as liable to be found in a sensory underload period as in its contrary. Its secret, I suspect, is human curiosity and/or frustration, and its etiology I wonder at. But Teg had seen pornography earlier, when she was about seven years old—presented as a negative example. Thus, it is hard for her to see it (she is on Pill 2) other than as ridiculousness, stupidity, and a general entropic condition. It is not conceptual. I, on the contrary, sometimes think that it is indeed conceptual. I remember medieval mystics attempting to set up communication which described their experience with God. Or someone as rhythmically/sexually aware of relationship with God as John Donne. Pornography is commonly rejected because it is publicly manifest in negative forms. Which makes one wonder if (however physical it is in display) it isn't as religious and conceptual in action as another approach, simply because it is so yearningly curious. How many of us can stand to be that curious? At least publicly? But this is Romantic; it is to think of Coleridge's "romantic chasm," etc. Which brings us to musicians, artists, and performing people.

When imaginative, creative people are mentioned in the manuscript, the reader gets the idea that these are societal engineers. They are economists, ecologists—scientists. Not a writer is mentioned, not an

Queries and Comments.

artist, or a musician. Music is generally mentioned, but as a device for instruction. It quite obviously can serve that function, but it also digs at the human core in such an OUTER (metaphysical) way that can't be matched by the OUTER language found *needed* in the world of 1994. I speak of the human being once more. I speak of the total man who includes intellect *and* emotion in his makeup. And to come at an improved world of 1994 by describing it as one which reduces emotion (Pill 2) or ignores it or denigrates it (as in the section on Artistia) is to overlook the value of perhaps the most powerful daimon in our psyche. How can ecology be totally concerned with the world without paying mind to emotion? How can sociofacts be so euphemistically referred to (ain't sex in there)? What is a community myth if it isn't (at least, also) emotion? One would suppose that an economist/ecologist would perceive of converting emotion, channeling it—harnessing it, not subverting it.

Though I respond to the perceptive and/or prophetic view of 1994, I remain a mite scared. It sometimes seems like a handbook for zombies or extremists. I would like to see more man in there. But, if I misunderstand, and have not properly participated in a participating book, let the above comments be that participation.

— —*Rex Worthington*
953 East Drive
Woodruff Place
Indianapolis, Indiana 46201

7

This is a "participation book" which focuses on the future; the reader is invited to write in comments, queries, and additions. The mimeoed pages with two inches of empty space labeled Queries and Comments allow the reader to co-author with no guilty pangs over writing in a book.

Functional is the world Teg documents. She is an Orwell Scholar in 1994, devoting a year to study the changes society has undergone in twenty-five years. The book is a set of documents to and from Teg which describes and comments on her progress. The authors anticipate no reader will find a utopia here since Teg finds many flaws in her society. In fact, it is a rather dreary and ex-

Queries and Comments. tremely utilitarian world—no humor or pleasure, even child's play is useful. However, the main disappointment is the authors' failure to describe a convincing world, to give a sense of time and place. Partly this is Teg's fault: her ability to communicate her perceptions is limited; and her style in no way distinguishes her from any of the people she interviews or from whom she receives letters. The obvious artificiality of certain documents detracts from the authenticity, which is found in similar books such as Capek's *War with the Newts*.

Surpassing the contents is the form; a communication from Theobald, Scott, and others simulating a communication from a "Synergy Document" which communicates Teg's notes on communication to which the reader is invited to communicate. The book does fulfill its function; few can resist the opportunity to participate; and the authors do focus on several interesting ideas about the future.

Unbound in form and design, *Teg's 1994* will probably change, reflecting the responses of readers. Like the documents in Teg's world, it is open for revision and additions from new sources. This form will perplex libraries that are closed to unbound books that may be co-authored by every reader. But what better place for a book on the future of communication than in a library.

——*Mary Sassé, c/o Synergy, Bay Area Reference Center*
San Francisco Public Library
Civic Center
San Francisco, California 94102

8

What comes to my mind consistently through TEG is "communication," personal telephones, etc., instant feedback, real learning possibility, problem solving, instant resource....housing structured to this communication, wheel spokes, interrelation, and TEG seeing the need for a supplementary room where people could come together. The team approach. I have been in touch with architect friends about these structures and how they come about. It was related to me about some of the new movements in architecture as TEAM approaches and not individual ego's at people's expense.

Learning—I identified immediately with the methods in the book. The TV is of the utmost, and responsible for the change we see in the young today, for the good and the bad. Has to be supplemented with individual feedback with touchable people.

Invisible College—the structure needs more elaborating. I felt distant in the pages as to its role in terms of what it replaced. Is everything becoming visible or invisible, or is it a fluid interchange and fusion like when Rock Music and Folk Music become Folk-Rock? The purpose I see, research grants, guaranteed income, freedom to pursue.

Credit card and money flow—nothing was discussed about the cash outlay from the government. I guess that question brings about the most important question to me. The transition period of this new society. You expressed doubts in your previous book about the impact of the transition. I find that the foremost question in the minds of the revolutionists I run into: They ask about the transition, everything else is meaningless when they see people starving. I can see that too. This is the question.

Chemistry—I feel strongly about this. Regarding TEG's pill-taking to bring down the emotional level. I see into this far-reaching innovations and complications. You know, dependency, addiction, bringing your emotional states to points where emotions are destroyed in terms of enjoyment in emotional things. Chemistry is now doing this with many drugs, even the psychedelics, and will come to a point in the very near future where drugs may in essence control our lives for the good or bad. Surely nutritional advantages can be seen for proper diets. It is an optimistic adventure. There are many other specific areas where one can research. The mind, etc.....

Law enforcement, high officials, government structure, money sources?????

World Game Of Buckminster Fuller. Related to your economic restructuring.

Queries and Comments.

Religion and politics—are they part or an unpart of TEG's 1994?

Tape recorders for everybody, or something like that, to record thoughts at the moment and keep them for discussion. Diaries. Some kind of chronological listings to see your own growth. To study yourself, to evaluate change in that context.

Facilitator—an "enabler." I can dig it.

The need to be individual even in the midst of society and relationships. The ability to get lost once in awhile.

Apprentice relationships, the return to a feudal happening of the medieval centuries. This intrigued me.

> ——*Gary Sager*
> *1435½ Ridgeway*
> *Los Angeles, California 92006*

9

Teg's 1994 has circulated here. To Q, a psychiatrist, who is enthusiastic about your behavior-shaping ideas; and to C, botanist, who liked the travel-and-project change of emphasis in higher education. Both guys I would put in any 50-member General Staff for Humanity (which is what I think we need). Your greatest problem with *Teg's* may be your admirers—the ones who will see it as science-fiction instead of alternative-future. (We should start a conscious AF subdivision of SF.) Q was struck by your two new parties (Hamilton-Jefferson over again?). I wouldn't be surprised to see a "structuralist" coalition by 1972: guaranteed income (for the poor) plus a "no-tax" platform (i.e. "down with bookkeeping" for the rich.)

10

I very much appreciated receiving from you *Teg's 1994* and have now had the opportunity to integrate its thinking with my own.

In every important way, *Teg's 1994* has confirmed my own 'Outer' and has helped me tremendously by providing a systemic conceptual framework in which these ideas and feelings can now be translated into personal change and social action.

— —*Rochelle M. Corson*

Queries and Comments.

11

Well, I've just read *Teg's 1994* and found it a very decent sort of Utopia. Like Huxley's *Island*, Morris' *News from Nowhere*, it would be a nice place to live. You've even got an island for the baddies like Well's *Modern Utopia.* Not a bad job at all but I don't think Orwell would care for it because it dodges all the questions he asked. Read Chapter 12 of the *Road to Wigan Pier.* Teg would fit right into Sarban's "utopia" as the daughter of a Teutonic Knight instead of as the daughter of a scientist, so I don't see why you continue to discount the possibility of genocide and reversion to feudalism. Teg would look good in a riding habit, riding after hounds, her communicator bouncing behind her. What the hell are all the proles doing while Teg is being facilitated? Kurt Vonnegut comes up with an answer (joining fraternal orders like the Masons and Elks) in *Player Piano*. I hope that you will read Chapter 12 of Orwell's *Road to Wigan Pier.* You're just too doggone much of an intellectual.

But there are a lot of good points in Teg. Like you, I too foresee the abandonment of the university but for slightly different reasons. (I notice Teg still lives in an "achievement" society where the boys of invisible college give each other marks. Must be tremendous infighting and public relations campaigns to get good marks from one another since, obviously, professorships and fellowships are limited. Even Bucky Fuller wouldn't like invisible college—not even if it threw its doors (non-existent of course) open to every proletarian slob).

The French eco-economist's lecture—he is you of course—is really brilliant; nothing so well thought out in Utopian literature. Like Zamiatin, you also anticipate continued crises—no stasis; this is the common pitfall of Utopists and you avoid it with intelligence. The only really nasty thing was Artistia; you should have called it Bohemia. The discipline required to produce art is awesome. Bohemia produces very little art. In any book of prophecy or Utopian scheme what is left unsaid is always more important than what is said. These are just a few random thoughts on *Teg.* I liked it very well.

— —*Michael Calaghan*
2037 K Street
Lincoln, Nebraska 68510

12

The point I wanted to make about Teg was that you have ignored the plight of millions of workless proletarians and that your solution is applicable only to the superior types. *Teg's 1994* could only work if the bulk of the population were culled out and burned up in furnaces or some such solution. You don't know anything at all about proletarian life and that, as I see it, is the only criticism of an otherwise ingenious work.

— —*Michael Calaghan*
2037 K Street
Lincoln, Nebraska 68510

13

I have just finished *Teg's 1994* for the first time, and probably, like most readers, with our limited understanding, am both enthralled and disappointed.

— —*Don J. Dodsworth*
Franklin County Children's Services
Frank and Gantz Roads
Grove City, Ohio 42123

14

The encounter with this text appears to be one of the most exciting and significant events in my life. It suggests possible "next steps" where I had in recent years seen only 2 possibilities: total entropy—or—limited synergy at a terrible price (in human sacrifice). My comments are arranged as follows: PRO's, CON's, questions, conclusion.

PRO's

The material contains many extremely valuable ideas, each of which offers a significant potential improvement relevant to a negative situation in our society, and some of these ideas would even lead to improvements on themselves after implementation—excellent!

Queries and Comments.

I like the way the text is held "on course" (i.e. as near to potential reality as possible)—e.g. ending in the face of vast new problems to solve (instead of some kind of ultimate Golden Age), and maintaining awareness of continuing change.

The problem-solving institutes and communication networks do appear to offer a practicable alternative to the political ideologies which have plagued human society with their fake panaceas for far too long. I am not yet convinced that this would work well, but it looks possible.

I agree 100% with these approaches to educational reform.

The hypothetical economic system with its ecofacts and sociofacts sounds plausible, but has more implications than I can visualize after one reading. Some of the basics are incontestable, i.e. the elimination of artificial scarcity, recycling, cybernetic production, and flow-control by information of needs.

The linguistic/semantic developments are fascinating, and probably would lead to greater clarity and accuracy in information transmission. Rudimentary and fragmentary forms of the three modes already exist. In our world, it is conspicuous that most scientists' INTER already leaps international barriers with comparative ease. I feel that inter-community bridging in SITUATIONAL, which bothered Teg so much, is mainly a matter of selecting individuals; some individuals are less limited by the conditioning of their native environment than others. OUTER, on the other hand, presents (now) vast problems of interpersonal translation, even within one dialect or jargon-complex within one language.

Queries and
Comments.

CON's

The work desperately needs additional contributions on the human level (as opposed to the cultural-economic level, which is represented very adequately). This is not merely a question of the given personalities, which are of limited importance. It seems to me that vital aspects of humanity in general have been omitted. Humans are more diverse, warmer, more sensuous and less serious than the general treatment in this text would suggest.

It would be easy to classify Teg herself as a robot, except that a rather similar breed appeared "over there" in the Stalin era. Not the faintest spark of humor is to be found. Love is not portrayed in any shape or form, although there are statements that it is necessary. But—perhaps it was felt that the bare bones of the intellectual events were all that could be presented here.

My argument becomes urgent when we consider the ethical value judgments in the implied blanket condemnation of sensory gratification, sexual freedom, and artistic freedom. One of the first things I would hope from an ideal society would be the final burial of the cruel doctrines of Calvin and the other Puritans where they belong: together with the rest of the nerve gas and nuclear weapons.

I believe that "planners" should build on a broad base, to accommodate everyone with the minimum of intolerance. In a free society, it is possible and even probable that less than half of the population would opt for a lasting monogamous, heterosexual marriage relationship. It is incorrect to relegate the rest to the status of a leper colony.

Art receives the same treatment in "Teg" that it gets in most *totalitarian* states: "to be any good, it must be intimately related to the community myth." There are no objections to socially-oriented art, but all the other kinds of art are equally valid, I think.

People are diverse individuals. Even after removal of the bonds, stresses, and strains of money-controlled society, I believe they (future generations) would be just as diverse, perhaps even more so. It may prove possible (and in some cases desirable) to change this by genetic intervention or by the use of drugs, but this should be approached with caution. There is no objection to the handling of the "Pill 2 question" in "Teg".

Thinking in a calmer fashion about intolerance, it seems to me that there is a certain "range of balance" in human activities, rather similar to ecological balance. Just as aspirin is ineffective in minute quantities, useful in small quantities, and lethal in large. quantities, so there are limits to the utility of human involvement in activities, whether they be work, orgies, or meditation....At this time, I do not know of any acceptable approach to problems arising from overstepping these limits, other than voluntary decision by the individual (which should of course be backed up by the availability of all the relevant information.)

Concerning inter-regional conflict: Voluntary supply of goods and services to scarcity regions is ethically correct, but unlikely to prevent conflict or even reduce tensions, unless backed up by "something else" (WHAT???). The Romans tried this on the German tribes, and the Germans tried it on the Magyars several centuries later. Both times it achieved temporary truces and ended in total war.

QUESTIONS
After removal of the carrot-and-stick of the money economy, would enough people do enough work?

Would it be naive to expect cybernetic technology to absorb *all* the really unpleasant work? If it doesn't, who would do it, and why?

Would there be a psychological epidemic based on boredom?

CONCLUSION
All these comments are based on my first reading of "Teg", straight through. After mailing this, I shall re-read "Teg". Some sections need to be read several times, and pondered over. I am aware that my attitudes probably contain some obsolete elements,

Queries and Comments.

Queries and
Comments.

but I am *not committed* to these attitudes. They merely embody the best values and principles I have been able to find up till now.

Two projects are virtually incandescent in priority and capable of implementation—NOW!!!

1. Experimental approaches to the assembly of unperverted information (and media for making it accessible), perhaps including simulated games—to prepare for change, and possibly provide a vehicle for it.

2. Terran citizen movement.

——*Paul Shewan*
P.O. Box 3851
Phoenix, Arizona 85030

15

Teg's 1994: An Anticipation of the Near Future confronts any reviewer with a thorny question: How can one review a Rorschach-like presentation? The approach taken in this review is twofold: First, a series of statements is made about the contents of the book. Then, a series of comments about the significance of the book is given. Those who *must* experience *Teg's 1994* will find it, later if not sooner. Others are not addressed.

Teg is a girl of 20 who in 1994 receives a one-year fellowship from the Orwell Foundation, established in 1984 to celebrate man's survival of that much-dreaded year. During her year of worldwide travel, study and investigation, Teg "reviews" the history of previous years in a literary device akin to Bellamy's *Looking Backward*. Gradually and not without the pain of personal growth, Teg learns of the emergence during the 1970s of the Planning Party, accompanied by the collapse of many colleges and universities and the sustained decline of cities as ecological thinking displaces economic thought.

Critical events of the mid-seventies included a neo-Luddite revolt against smothering technology, as well as a consumer revolt and an increasing polarization between the have-not and have-got sectors of the earth. In the Scientists Synergy of 1979, some researchers refused to disseminate falsified or distorted information. The outcome of these events and trends in the early 1980s was the establishment in Hawaii of the Terran Communication Center, first of a series of terran centers devoted to various problem/possibility areas. Through the TCC, three fundamentally new communication styles—*inter, outer* and *situational*—were developed so that by the mid-1980s significant new modes of thinking and knowing emerged around the world, causing in the early 1990s a growing decline in social responsibility and a crisis in economic growth. There the book ends.

So much for the bare synopsis. In this context, British economist Theobald and his anthropologist wife have sketched the outlines of a theory of future economics, politics, cultural styles, and much more. Also suggested are the eternal stresses, strains, hopes, and disappointments generated in conflicts between the old and the new.

As a science fiction novel, *Teg's 1994* is rough, uneven and sometimes awkward. As an intellectual excursion into possible future societies, the book's organization and manner of treatment are not what one expects. In many ways, the ideas and values conveyed might be presented more forcefully on the motion picture screen— or even better, in a revised version of the computerized Delphi futures exploration system at the University of Illinois. In this way, particular implications could be explored in depth and alternative scenarios created according to the speculations of each experiencer.

Teg's 1994 ultimately is not a book. It is a vehicle through which the authors—and there were many besides the two whose names appear, as is gladly acknowledged by them—can share a vision, a spirit, and a call to community to all those who have rejected the notion of competition as the primary organizing principle of society. *Teg's 1994* asserts that rich, diverse, and above all *real* communion can be achieved via collaboration in new

Queries and Comments.

ways whose outlines already are perceptible. In the style of the Old World, this review would conclude: *Teg's 1994* is an *important* book. Read it! In New World style, let us part rather on the following note: Here is one small clearing in the wilderness where those of us in the Way can find each other.

— —David Miller
908 Fox Plaza
San Francisco, California 94102

16

A glimpse there—eleven people blowing grass; next slide—seven people in a rowboat; now a sister flying in a tree, but turn the knob and three geese and a gander float by. Be cautious—we're surrounded ourselves. We try to reach out to express and discover ourselves, but I feel blocked at so many turns. Those people—how do I relate to them? What do we have in common? How will I understand what they have to say? how will they understand what i have to say? Expression, medium, words, symbols: mind fuck.

People to relate to; also high around me are piles of books and magazines and slides and movies—so many neatly catalogued and indexed mounds. So much information—so many thoughts—they grow higher each day. Will I have any time to do anything except search?

I'm sorry Mary, *Teg's 1994* does not speak to me about the future, it speaks about now. 1994 is not a temporal period; it is a spirit of mind. While Theobald and Scott offer some interesting conceptions of future institutions, I understand the main focus of the book to be mediums of intercourse.

We begin to analyze something—maybe an action, maybe a thought, maybe something you said or thought or did. We define the problem, find terms whose usage we understand and begin. Our analysis is hooked into a conceptual framework with a hook which we use as a handle: we analyze *vis-a-vis* that framework. We have logical thoughts—but what we analyze slips more into the framework and further from us. We can put the object of our analysis into perspective.

Wait—something happened—the framework just turned into a box, and we're inside. The problems we've been discussing exist only within that framework which defines them. The framework defines itself too—it's not open to our logical analysis. But now, just now something happened, and we need to get beyond the framework; it's served us well until now, but we've got to move beyond.

So we let our minds wander—hook them on to a breeze and fly like kites, we slip past the framework—we're not logical now because logic only exists in frames. We abandon our preconceptions and barriers and voice thoughts that we don't understand ourselves —we help each other extend and develop them. Sometimes new patterns and frameworks emerge. . .

But that's rough too. Sure, it's nice to let your mind wander, but even that can become a chore, a duty. Sometimes we've got to *IS*. We've got to let it all down and not analyze or wander and just be where we are and feel and enjoy it. We've got to be with people we love and trust—people with whom we share certain perceptions of reality. We communicate by touch—by sense—by feel. When I'm with my people we know enough about each other that we can accept each other and *IS*. Please touch someone today.

Teg works with these three mediums of expression—she calls them INTER, OUTER, and SITUATIONAL. She comes to learn new things about their potentials and limitations because of the way in which she experiences them. I experienced it with her.

Everywhere there's more oozing in; splat! There's a new drop on the pile. We keep talking and writing and uncovering new facts and fantasies. Where and how and when do they all fit it? Hand me a shovel and turn the knob; we've got to move. It's not enough to simply classify and divide into piles—each one of us has to find the information which has personal value. We need to create synergenic movements: paths to higher levels of integration and understanding.

I don't want distinctions to dissolve problems. So many times we make symbols for distinctions which are made by the symbols. I

Queries and Comments.

Queries and Comments. can't perceive the nature of a whole thing by looking at parts which are without real distinction. We need synergenic exchanges—not euthropic falsifications of reality.

Teg begins to deal with the piles—to sort her way through—to perceive the need for new systems of information exchange. She doesn't have the answers; we have to discover them together. She does begin to show some of the problems.

Move along with Teg. If you need to analyze everything Theobald and Scott say—do that later. Now, let your mind wander and OUTER around. Sisters and brothers, don't read *Teg's 1994*; interact with it. Let it carry and carry it.

Stimulation of new thoughts and responses. Struggle, love, create!
——Robert Stiltger
Radical Research Center
Carleton College
Northfield, Minnesota 55057

17

I must give you my reaction at this point to *Teg*: it was exciting and a bit scary. I think I know your writing well enough to know that what I am going to say is assumed by you to be going on in Teg and you simply didn't have enough room to put it in. I kept looking for the joy, the happiness—of course, I didn't find it. Why not insert a couple of record entries on Teg's experience while off Pill 2. Do you know I had to go to George Leonard's *Education and Ecstasy* to get my perspective back.

——Pete Fisher
18085 Birchcrest
Detroit, Michigan 48221

18

. . .we've just got around to 1994 in the utopia class, so I can tell you something on how it goes. As you see from the set-up described in the syllabus, the class is organized around a presentation of 3 societal models in fiction (in turn based on Joan Lewis' analysis). 1994 then is most useful as a wrapup to this part of the course, before the students take over class presentations, as it provides a framework for us to discuss how the various models we've read previously might work in Teg's world; my assumption is that the freedom from material needs enables people to establish whatever situations they desire, without interfering with other groups' similar right. Thus, we have discussed possible community relations among communities based on myths similar to those found (or which we might read into) such books as "Walden II" (behaviorism), "Anthem" (free enterprise—Artistia?), & "Island" (humanistic, mystical). Our thoughts agree with yours, that community relations would become quite chaotic indeed, perhaps leading to another cycle of the makings of states again—communities of like mind banding together to ward off supposed common enemies. We've also simulated a few of the situations you postulate; since my class is made up of seniors at Case Tech (one of several social science courses they must take), it seemed most appropriate to have them act through the Scientists Synergy; they turned out to be hesitant about risking their "job" security by blowing the whistle on secret info, as we played through this notion, but could see following the lead of famous types; they also resisted the notion that scientists & engineers must be held primarily responsible for the effects of their gadgets.

You might also be interested in some of the criticisms of 1994 as a scenario: are we seeing only the elite of Teg's world, and if so, what is the life of the common man like? It's not clear how the neo-Luddite stage ends. You seem to presume great rationality by people (that they will agree to sweeping institutional change once shown the benefits). With all the great value changes, people seem to get married & have children as we do (i.e., corresponding changes in family/social life?). Somewhere along the line, it isn't clear how the threat of mass war was eliminated—who's running the inspection teams?

——*Dennis Livingstone*
Case Western Reserve University
Cleveland, Ohio 44106

19

While science fiction has not been noted for dwelling on positive

utopias, it may be that we are in for a comeback of this *genre*
thanks to the precepts of futures studies. If it is vital for society
to have some picture of the array of possible futures from which
to choose the direction of its growth, it is most helpful for some
of these pictures to present models of the most desirable society
that the authors can imagine on the basis of presently known
trends. *Teg's 1994* becomes doubly interesting because it is a
utopia writtten at the close of the 1960s, forcing the authors to
take account in their model of the disruptive trends so harshly
revealed during that decade.

The result is a fascinating portrait, depicted through a series of "documents" written or collected by the heroine, which would seem to
represent a society based on strands from the new left/hippie philosophy of decentralization. This possible world of 1994 is one in
which "the techno-system acts merely as infra-structure, expansion
and growth are no longer goals and human society has re-
emphasized social interaction through world-wide decentralization
into small, sub-cultural communities". Thanks to a global communications network, the trend towards concentrated urbanization is reversed and, with the help of a new profession of "community facilitators", individuals group themselves voluntarily into "consentives"
in which maximally supportive environments for self-development
can be created. Each community is based on different founding
myths, goals, and behavior patterns, making for rich cultural
diversity. A cybernated production system has resulted in the
elimination of a money economy in the more prosperous regions;
education is composed of programmed teaching, self-guidance,
group interaction, and apprenticeships. It is not a perfect world,
however, and at the end the characters realize that the community movement has gone so far as to result in global entropy as
individuals no longer are able to communicate easily across community lines.

For myself, there are some large conceptual gaps in the book that
do not enhance credibility of such a society. Nothing at all is said
about what happens to the multi-billion dollar war economy or
how the great international issues just fade away in the face of
prosperity. The form of government is never very clear, but appears

to be a kind of benevolent, technocratic elite that knows "what's best" for the world. On the whole, I am doubtful that so many people could behave so rationally as the story must assume they do for its world to be possible.

Queries and Comments.

> — —*Dennis Livingstone*
> *Case Western Reserve University*
> *Cleveland, Ohio 44106*

20

Two things happened this week which suddenly brought to me a perfect analogy which will, I think, help to communicate to you how I see, in general, the problems and virtues of *Teg's 1994*. Arthur Clarke was in town and Mort and I were invited, with a mutual friend, to have dinner with him. Alas, I had (of all things) a PTA commitment and only Mort and his wife could go. The movie 2001 also came back to Chicago and my son went to see it for the second time. Both these events evoked discussion and re-discussion about 2001. Suddenly last night my analogy came to me. Folk respond to 2001 in at least three basic ways: 1. They don't care much for it; it is dull, confusing or meaningless. 2. They find it mildly interesting, not dull, but not terribly exciting. 3. They go wild over it; they become cultists about it. *Teg's 1994* is like 2001. My response to both ranges somewhere between #1 and #2, but I cannot deny the very favorable response of many. . . .

If I would make a generalization I would say this: The work has lots of darn good stuff in it, a few nice touches of technique, and it is a brilliant *idea* (people often say to me that they love the idea of the novel and their anticipation of it but in fact find the paragraph describing the novel in the Working Appendix to *Alternative Future* more interesting than the novel), but overall the work is dull/boring, unimaginative and gimmicky. . . .

. . .I would also suggest that ironically/paradoxically *Teg's 1994* is the sort of work such as *I* should write and not you. That's what disappoints me about it. It falls short of its conception. . . .

> — —*Durrett Wagner*
> *Swallow Press*
> *1139 S. Wabash Avenue*
> *Chicago, Illinois 60605*

Queries and Comments.

21

I reread *Teg's 1994* during my free time of the summer term and found that my opinions had not changed but had simply become more generalized. I plan on rereading in December.

Whenever I'm at the Laundromat doing my non-instant-clean and non-recyclable clothing I longingly think of the days when 1 may no longer need to waste time doing such an unending and mean- ingless task. There are so many other more important things to which I could and would love to devote myself. Your whole sec- tion on politics definitely seems to be coming true. Election 1970 was a clear indication of more liberalism leading towards the ulti- mate chaos.

— —Arlene Crandall
7405 North Hoyne
Chicago, Illinois

22

We live in a time when the only predictable thing about the future of one generation hence is that it will be utterly unlike the world we know now. We have the power to choose our future. This being the case, there are few more important activities at the present time than the construction of feasible and ethically acceptable visions of the future. *Teg's 1994* is a brilliantly heuristic attempt at future writing and should go far to influence the future we choose.

— —David Clarke
Western Washington State College
Bellingham, Washington 98225

23

At the risk of having you take the enclosures in this letter and dumping them into the wastebasket without further ado I must say that the book disappointed me. In your *1994*—although not necessarily elsewhere—your perceptions are at one place while mine are at another. We share similar values but our eyes are in two very different heads. Let me explain.

The "school" you portray maximizes human freedom and attempts to facilitate personal maturation by its design. It has the purposes of some of the great utopias—which is laudable. The world becomes a classroom and life stages become "grades," if that rough equivalent isn't altogether misleading. What is there to say except "how soon?"

But there is this to consider: somehow Teg combines *Up the Down Staircase*, Bellamy, Friends World College, McLuhan, and *Walden Two* without transcending them, i.e., without convincing the reader, and maybe others, that it *could* work that way (I already agree that it *should*.) Take Bellamy, for instance. The success of the Planning Party in 1972 sounds very much like the rise of the National Party in *Looking Backward* and the credibility of the prophecy is now quite low. Samuel Lubell wasn't the last political futurist to comment about the durability of the party system, and the vision of the political future he paints was altogether overlooked in *1994.* Why, for example, is there no extensive reflection about the coming of age of the "baby boom"? That, to my mind, is the most powerful force for change in the future—for the next 20 years anyhow—than any diversionary tactics of today's adults. And not only politically. Look at what the young have already done to: (A) films, (B) music, and (C) clothing and hair styles. Next, although not in this order, probably, will come (1) business reorganization, especially in the lower echelons (á la Warren Bennis or Townsend), then (2) housing styles, (3) broadcasting fare, and (4) reorganization of the social order, bit-by-bit, so that law, politics, etc. become different species than they are now. Not only do the young have numbers—almost 50,000,000 were born in the 1946-1960 boom years—but they also are the carriers of, in Paul Goodman's phrase, a "new reformation." To get to where Teg got would require such a reformation and the force of the millions of young, but *1994* uses another hypothesis in explaining future history and, to me, seems less credible as a result.

— —*Billy Rojas*
School of Education
University of Massachusetts
Amherst, Massachusetts 01022

24

Personal Attitude: Listening to music; partially relaxed after exhila-
rating day of investigating sewage treatment plant.

I probably should have read *Teg* over once more to get my
attitudes about it straightened out. Here is my reaction and general
comment summary.

My most general comment has a lot to do with the style of the
book, and I'm only concerned about it because I found several
friends were turned off by it. You say near the end that "if you're
going to create new patterns they should be signalled by new descriptors"—I understand that people get hung up by semantics more
than anything and that new words are usually essential to overcome this communication barrier—but I think use of new descriptors was (is) a little overdone in *Teg's*. The result is an "unread-
ability" quality that makes the reading sometimes monotonous.
After I looked up most of the words, it made a lot more sense
and was easier to get into, but for most people—well you know.

The scenes also seem a little on the cold side and this is ironic
since the whole thing is supposed to be centered around terran
socialization. Maybe a good environmental writer could contribute
a couple of more environmentally-oriented scenes.. I would help to
make the book more readable for people who get depressed by
concrete and I do. Maybe I just didn't read carefully or something,
but the settings seem to have a metallic, 1984 type quality.

I thought that *Teg's* was an excellent attempt (99% success) to create
a participatory analysis out of the process of reading the book.
In fact, I think it will come as a shock to people who read books
so they can ingest an opinion. *Teg's* forces you to formulate an
opinion or go away confused. It bothered me at times not to be
able to discern what your opinions actually are, but it doesn't
really matter. It wasn't until the end of the third section that I
realized how objective you had actually been and it was very
refreshing.

I'm not that familiar with cybernation and the technical aspects
of it, and I think a section describing a trip by Teg to an ecofact

production site would be helpful here. You ought to get Illich to write a more detailed account of the de-schooling process which could be related by one of the historians—maybe B. (Illich was also at Iowa State.) I can't believe that's going to happen in 2 years.

Your (?) comment about the young and the *women* "coming to understand the implications of recent research on mechanisms of thought" was quite enlightening. Do you think there may be/are biological reasons or is it socialization? Could be both.

I found the language set-up quite disturbing from the start and was not surprised at the end: good development though.

Artistia could be more amusing and supportive of the book as a whole if elaborated. You could possibly go into the condition of their environment.

I haven't made up my mind yet whether I believe people can function humanly *without* some form of government, whether it be at the international or sub-cultural terran level. You mentioned how *governments* were creating programs of preventative medicine, etc. —What governments??

As I am rapidly becoming a vegetarian, I would like to see a section explaining the fact that protein is synthesized and steak etc. is really artificial in 1994. I found myself wondering what the "high dishes" consist of.

Would it be a fair guess to say that you believe the transitory periods as described by the historians are *necessary* to achieve synergy?

I've learned a lot since I came to Iowa State University—as a result of the communication potentials by no means a part of the "institution"—most importantly that I am too idealistic to be able to cop-out by taking drugs, conforming, or hermitization. Many of my close friends have come home from school so depressed that they have given up on man, and that has disturbed me. Iowa State is probably for me the most frustrating place on earth, and I don't

Queries and Comments. know if I can function there much longer. The people are *so* apathetic I get depressed thinking about it. And I'm not talking about the general apathy that pervades everywhere on campus—this is really *super-apathy.* Even Environmental Action is talking about having a mickey mouse *fair* for Earth Week.

Do you have any suggestions as to how I can get actively involved with promoting and bringing about the new world now? Do you think it would be best to stay in school to help "tear down from within" to use a cliche? It's already 1971 and no ABCs to speak of.

I was really impressed by the way you can put down in words ideas I've had drifting around my cortex but could never quite write down. I hate to say that I think *Teg's* could be a handbook for the future—but I think it's getting close.

— —*J. A. Boeger*
2717 West Street
Ames, Iowa 50010

25

To add to my prior comments (actually non-comments) on *Teg*, I would like to say that I read *The Republic* by Plato and J.S. Mill almost simultaneously with *Alternative Future* and *Teg.* It would really be great if everyone could do that. I'm a freshman in college, Iowa State University, and so I haven't had quite enough living prime time to arrange my beliefs and ideas into a coherent philosophy. I must say that all of this in a matter of four months has been a mind-altering experience. I said in a prior letter that I had "learned a lot." That was an understatement. I have had more truth realizations in recent months than in the preceding 18 years. I guess that's not freaky or anything, but it's fantastic.

It took me a while to completely understand the message at the beginning of section III of *Teg*—that everything not in the process of being born is dying—that is probably going to be the hardest truth for man to comprehend. Sitting here, they're going to say —"Shit, you can't climb forever, that's an impossibility." People are probably going to reject the idea because they're afraid there won't be any plateaus to rest upon. I guess somebody will have to convince them—if they can't convince themselves—that gravity actually pulls things up—the past and fear of the future are the only chains which are pulling us down.

I'm right in the middle of Mill's theory on Utilitarianism, and how the concept of sapiential authority fits in is beautiful. I think that even though Plato seems like a bastard to most people because of his class society, I believe he was just on an ego trip and really knew what he was talking about (what he believed got distorted by his vanity.) I hope that never happens to you or your friends. That's the true value of history—we can look back and say *that* was the mistake which stifled the world.

I think I'll make this a continuing letter so I can put down more things as they come. For me *Teg* will be a continuum of realization—I can't possibly understand and truly realize everything at once. If you think I'm doing this for you to print then there is no love here. Love is trust. I shouldn''t even have written that because it shows that I too have an inner feeling of distrust. That's really shitty and I hope to overcome all distrust of everyone. I'll probably get killed or something, but I don't care, because if I can't live love I don't want to live at all.

— —J. A. Boeger
2717 West Street
Ames, Iowa 50010

26

About *Teg's 1994*. It sits on our desk. And I browse through it from time to time. Never have had the need to swallow it whole, but frequently like to make contact. Dig the form more and more. Always tantalized by the curiosity of an artifact of the future. The style is often more intriguing than the content. I have a hard time getting my head into thinking on a national policy level lately. Mostly into becoming a resident of Manhattan. Broader thinking usually is in a world context. Bucky Fuller and the Whole Earth Catalog people have got me. Haven't had any experience with the World Game yet, but I think a lot about what it would mean to be a local focus for such a thing.

Queries and Comments.

The one fantasy in *Teg's* which most turned me on was the strategy the young scientists used to gain enough power to make information free. The strike coupled with income sharing. Felt right on. I keep thinking that income sharing on some fairly large scale is essential to building the movement work that needs to be done in the next ten years both inside and outside the system. I have a fantasy of catalyzing a group of faculty and other young professionals in Manhattan into an income sharing group. Say, putting 10% of their income into a fund, 5% of which would build as an insurance fund in case any of them got fired. Another 5% would go to supporting people working outside the system on subsistence. The faculty need this kind of security to take the personal and political risks to get together. The people outside need this kind of commitment and support from people inside to really get into full-time work towards nonviolent alternatives. . . .I might add that the problem in creating such an income sharing strategy is not mainly financial. Building community and relationships of deeper personal and political trust would lead to money and resource sharing. I am just beginning to realize that I had my strategy before my goals, or at least hadn't grokked their inter-relatedness.

— —*Phil Werdell*

27

I recently read *Teg's 1994* and have made some observations concerning it. Although I am in complete agreement with the main ideas presented, I find the tone and attitude of the book very disturbing.

First, the attitude of the book is extremely clinical. The characters are terribly dispassionate and analytical. They exhibit few emotions. I think it would be very appropriate here to reiterate two paragraphs from *Thus Spoke Zarathustra:*

> And when I beheld my devil, I found him serious, thorough profound, solemn; it was the Spirit of Gravity—through him all things are ruined.

> One does not kill by anger but by laughter. Come, let us kill the Spirit of Gravity!

Second, everything is too ordered. The Apollonian structure is stifling and the "business" attitude is all-encompassing. Even the entertainment and celebrations, which are also designed to educate, are horribly ordered and unfestive.

I honestly believe a bit of the Dionysian spirit would have added a great sense of freedom, spontaneity, creativity, and joy.

— —*Catherine Johnson*
1805 Ohio Road
Brookings, South Dakota 57006

Queries and Comments.

28

Until Cathy pointed out the matter, this characteristic of the work had never occurred to me, i.e., that it is overly rationalistic to the exclusion of the other, more emotional dimensions of human life.

I'm not sure I feel the force of the criticism very much so as to share it as a serious defect. One reason is that most dionysian types I've run into I don't find too impressive, if "by their fruits you shall know them" is any criterion. I see little sense of a viable external world and society in them, but rather a symptom of the absence of this and what it can produce. Also, they do not seem able to produce a politics of the dionysion exhuberation. In this connection, I am somewhat suspicious of "holy madness", N.O. Brown, Laing, *et al*. (I don't mean to imply Cathy means to say so, or even is drawing on this background.)

Another factor is that the task "Teg" is involved in is terribly demanding, and leaves little time for fun and games, anymore than does the M.D. internship year. Also, the internal life of the various decentralized communities is not shown to us.

More important is my own dionysion response to the work, i.e., the eyeopening vision of an alternative society and the fundamental rightness, sense, reality of it. It leaves me terribly moved and excited.

Perhaps the heart of it all is the *kind* of reason and thought which dominates the work. It *is* extremely rational, critical, but not in

Queries and Comments. that objective (subject/object) sense usually meant. Rather, it manifests (I think) that principle of the suspended judgement, working from the effect back, planned intervention, which represents a new *kind* of human reason. In a real sense this is *thoroughly* subjective and runs the range of emotional involvement. The line: "the joy and pain of synergistic insight" has real force for me. I think I've known it. Also, as expressly dealt with in the work, is there not some benefit in learning to control the emotional element, when it becomes intrusive?

Nevertheless, I think there is some genuine force in what Cathy says. It is a bit *too* serious (but not sterile hardly!), *too* strained, overly serious, "clinical" (but *not* detached), and lacking a bit in the "vital juices." Either we have a new kind of human person, or I have missed something in the work, or the work itself is missing something.

— —*David Fee*
University of South Dakota
Brookings, South Dakota

29

As I write this, I have just finished *The Economics of Abundance*, having read *Teg's 1994* a few weeks ago. Wonder if you know that *Teg's* comes much more clear after reading *Abundance.* Many of the concepts in *Teg's* left me puzzled until I read *Abundance*. I guess my only worthwhile comment to *Teg's* is simply a notion that there are so many new concepts and ideas in it that you would have to be a Theobald reader first, a *Teg's* reader afterwards. How many of those who have liked *Teg's* have read your other work? I really was fascinated by it. It was to me like a document that I found in the future which had been brought back for me to pore over.

——*Ralph Brent*

AUTHOR'S COMMENTS

The spoken and written responses received could be analyzed and discussed in many ways. The following comments touch briefly on some of the points raised in the responses, and then give some of our own views on the future and relate them to reader response.

Queries and Comments.

One rather general complaint was the use of little-known or invented words:

> My most general comment has a lot to do with the style of the book, and I'm only concerned about it because I found several friends were turned off by it. You say near the end that 'if you're going to create new patterns they should be signalled by new descriptors.' I understand that people get hung up by semantics more than anything and that new words are usually essential to overcome the communications barrier—but I think the use of new descriptors was (is) a little overdone in *Teg's*. The result is an 'unreadability' quality that makes the reading sometimes monotonous. After I'd looked up most of the words, it made a lot more sense, and was easier to get into. . .(Response 24)

The most general reaction has been against what is perceived as a lack of emotion, humanity, and passion in the book. This type of comment occurs again and again. A few readers, however, went behind the surface character of the book, and of Teg herself, and saw a deeper possibility of creativity and joy.

> . . .the society outlined reminds me of a kind that Orwell might create but to which he wouldn't subscribe. It sounds as sterile as the political, or economist/ecologist language which describes it. . . I would make [the book] more human. (Response 6)

189

Queries and
Comments.
In fact, it is a rather dreary and extremely utilitarian world —no humor or pleasure, even child's play is useful. (Response 7)

The work desperately needs additional contributions on the human level. . . Humans are more diverse, warmer, more sensuous and less serious than the general treatment in this text would suggest. (Response 14)

Sure it's nice to let your mind wander, but even that can become a chore, a duty. . .Teg works with three. . .mediums of expression—she calls them INTER, OUTER, and SIT-UATIONAL. She comes to learn new things about their potentials and limitations because of the way she experiences them. I experienced it with her. (Response 16)

I kept looking for the joy, the happiness: of course I didn't find it. (Response 17)

The scenes also seem a little on the cold side and this is ironic since the whole thing is supposed to be centered a-round terran socialization. (Response 24)

I honestly believe that a bit of the Dionysian spirit would have added a greater sense of freedom, spontaneity, creativity and joy. (Response 27)

More important is my own dionysian response to the work: i.e. the eyeopening vision of an alternative society and the fundamental rightness, sense, reality of it. It leaves me terribly moved and excited. (Response 28)

Some readers still found the book "Utopian," despite our warning in the mimeographed preface: "We do not anticipate that any reader will find his ideal future society mirrored in this book because this is not a Utopian description. *Teg's 1994* sketches a possible future where the techno-system acts merely as infrastructure, expansion and growth are no longer goals and human society has reemphasized social interaction through worldwide decentralization into small, sub-cultural communities."

Well, I've just read *Teg's 1994* and found it a very decent   *Queries and*
sort of Utopia. Like Huxley's *Island*, Morris's *News from*   *Comments.*
Nowhere, it would be a nice place to live. (Response 11)

Others felt that we had underestimated the power of science and
technology to change man:

The image of MAN as opposed to the image of men both
psychologically and physically (color) is certainly bound
to undergo greater changes due to genetic interference, much
before 1994, yet this does not seem to enter in as a consideration in the discussions of 'cultural divergence.' (Response 4)

A fundamental area of disagreement among readers was the type
of learning that *Teg's 1994* would facilitate:

"Your greatest problem with Teg's may be your admirers
—the ones who will see it as science-fiction instead of alternative-future. (Response 9)

We need a seed to get the crystal growing. (Response 24)

I am just beginning to realize that I had my strategy before
my goals, or at least hadn't grokked [fully understood] their
interrelatedness. (Response 26)

I identified immediately with the methods in the book. (Response 8)

If it is vital for society to have some picture of the array
of possible futures from which to choose the direction of its
growth, it is most helpful for some of these pictures to present models of the most desirable society that authors
can imagine on the basis of presently known trends. (Response 19)

We have the power to choose our future. This being the case
there are few more important activities at the present time

Queries and Comments. than the construction of feasible and ethically acceptable visions of the future. *Teg's 1994* is a brilliantly heuristic attempt at future writing and should go far to influence the future we choose. (Response 22)

But there is this to consider: somehow Teg combines *Up the Down Staircase,* Bellamy, Friends World College, McLuhan and *Walden Two* without transcending them, i.e. without convincing this reader, and maybe others, that it *could* work that way. (I already agree that it *should.*) Take Bellamy, for instance. The success of the Planning Party in 1972 sounds very much like the rise of the National Party in *Looking Backward* and the credibility of the prophecy is now quite low. (Response 23)

My own research and observations have convinced me that the human seeks learning actively. One must only make the materials available. (Response 2)

The point I wanted to make about *Teg's* was that you have ignored the plight of millions of workless proletarians and that your solution is applicable only to the superior types. (Response 12)

I like the way the text is held on course (i.e. as near to potential reality as possible)—e.g. ending in the face of vast new problems to solve (instead of some kind of ultimate Golden Age) and maintaining awareness of continuing change. (Response 14)

They [readers who were seniors at Case Tech] turned out to be hesitant about risking their "job" security by blowing the whistle on secret information. . .but could see following the lead of famous types; they also resisted the notion that scientists and engineers must be held primarily responsible for the effects of their gadgets. (Response 18)

I guess somebody will have to convince them—if they can't convince themselves—that gravity actually pulls things up

—the past and fear of the future are the only chains which
are pulling us down. (Response 24)

* *   * *   * *

Teg's 1994, like all writing, is based on a particular world view.
It differs profoundly from the two patterns which are predomin-
nantly used in analyzing the future at the present time—those used
by the extrapolators and those used by the creatists. (For a definition and expansion of these terms, see *Habit and Habitat*,
Robert Theobold, 1972).

The extrapolators assume that the future will continue the trends
which are already apparent. They argue that we should expect no
fundamental change in man's assumptions, his thinking, or his
style of life in the remainder of the century. They believe, therefore,
that those who are trying to bring about change are naive or
destructive.

Until recently, this was the only commonly acceptable way of looking at the future. The Commission on the Year 2000, Herman
Kahn, Daniel Bell and, most recently, Alvin Toffler have set out
the assumptions and the conclusions of this school of thought. Man
has already made his future, the analysts argue, now he must
adapt to what he has created.

The assumption of the unchangeability of trends into the future is
shared by another group which at first sight would appear to be
diametrically opposed. Such groups as Students for a Democratic
Society—and their later offshoot, Weathermen;—also act on the
belief that the future, as extrapolation of the present, cannot be
changed. But while Kahn, Bell, and Toffler find this reality acceptable, SDS and the Weathermen see this reality as being so dis-
astrous that they claim the right to cut off all the trends, pull down
the total system, and thus save Western man from the fate which
presently lies ahead of him.

During the sixties, a change in the way of thinking about the future
began to develop. People started to believe that their future was

not totally constrained by the inevitable development of all existing
trends—that it was possible to create the world *they wanted*. A
growing number of individuals began to act as though the future
—at least their personal future—was alterable. Instead of trying to
tear down the existing system, they chose to set up alternative
models for the future combining some existing trends with some
new ones. The creation of communes and free stores, free universities and "alternative" newspapers are all part of this movement.
Those who are participating in it are the "creatists."

Charles Reich's *The Greening of America* is the best-known statement of this viewpoint. Significant changes, he argues, depend upon
an alteration in consciousness. When a change in consciousness does
take place, fundamental alterations in socioeconomic patterns are
inevitable.

Reich's view is reasonable. Men inevitably act on the basis of their
perceived self-interest: any change in the way people understand the
world in which they live changes their perceived self-interest. Reich
all too often assumes, however, that the conclusions people will
reach on the basis of a change in consciousness will necessarily
be beneficial. In effect, he assumes that change, and even innovation,
are inevitably for the better.

In reality, an examination of the experience of the creatists is highly
discouraging. It is this group which is caught up in the neo-Luddite revolt rather than in trying to perceive how to use the new
technology humanly. It is also this group which assumes that all
of man's problems can be solved by good-will rather than by
facing up to the extraordinary effort and imagination needed to
ensure synergy. If we are to create situations in which the desires
of the individual and the needs of the society are to be congruent,
we shall require far higher levels of organization than we have yet
achieved.

In effect, the extrapolators and the creatists are refighting the classic
battle between extreme concepts of determinism and extreme concepts of free will. The extrapolators deny that any action can alter
the future ahead of us. The creatists, on the other hand, argue that

there are no constraints to prevent man from inventing *any* future that he desires.

It is this dualism which has always torn Western man. He has seen himself at one extreme as a free spirit above any form of restraint or coercion. At the other extreme, he has seen himself as a plaything of the gods, buffeted by fate. The survival of Western man depends on the elimination of this dualism—and indeed the contradictions which it has caused in our thought processes and our languages.

Teg's 1994 attempts to bring these extreme views together in a yin-yang balance: to recognize the elements of truth in Western man's belief in *both* determinism *and* free will. Determinism obviously underestimates man's power to influence his future; free will equally obviously overestimates it.

How then can we appraise our potentials and our limitations? Each human being is restricted to perceiving a part of the total reality with which he is surrounded. Some of our limitations are genetic —and genetic change would certainly produce other limitations. Some are cultural: all cultures impose limitations, and it is our culture which permits us to manifest our humanity. Some result from the fact that we have limited input-channels and that we can only receive a certain amount of information within a given amount of time.

Each human being determines the future he can create by his screening of his perceptions. However, it must never be forgotten that the ability of the individual to act on his perceptions is constrained by his physical world: Leonardo da Vinci could imagine airplanes but he could not build them because the necessary technology did not exist. The effectiveness of a human being does not only depend on his dreams, but also on his ability to realize them. A poor man in the scarcity-regions of the world does not have the same potentials as an individual living within the abundance-regions.

The way in which each person sees reality determines the areas in which they can operate effectively. When we choose to open our

senses and our minds to certain types of information, we inevitably
will change our perception of the world—and with it our perceived
self-interest. By deciding which areas of reality we shall permit to
enter our lives and those we shall screen out, we determine the
possibilities for our further development. Some possibilities which
could have existed we shall never discover because our self-chosen
pattern of perceptions will effectively have screened them out.

In addition, the ability to create change depends on the sensitivity
of an individual to the views of those with whom he works and his
ability to enable them to discover the opportunity for a better future.
Synergetic change cannot be forced—it requires the consent of those
involved in the situation.

It is those readers already seeking synergy who can gain most from
Teg's 1994. They can take what they need from the book and
apply it to what is already important to them. The book will not
supply a new purpose in life or a new view of the world. We hope
however, that it will be a useful tool in developing clearer perceptions of reality—the essential step toward a synergetic future.

> The problems encountered in the small sub-cultural com-
> munities will yield to solutions. The change you have en-
> visioned is not ideal in all aspects but it is a plausible and
> livable situation. The main problem seems to be to avoid
> entropic situations. Entropies are what originally caused
> the turmoil of the sixties but Teg shows foresight in plan-
> ing a meeting toward the creation of a joint synergy myth
> to prevent a repetition of entropic situations. There seems to
> be hope for the human race. (Response 1)

> *Teg's 1994*. . .is not a temporal period; it is a spirit of mind.
> (Response 6)

> I very much appreciated receiving from you *Teg's 1994* and
> have now had the opportunity to integrate its thinking with
> my own. (Response 10)

> *Teg's 1994*. . .sits on our desk. And I browse through it

from time to time. Never had the need to swallow it whole, but frequently like to make contact. (Response 26)

Now that *Teg's 1994* is printed, what are our expectations for growth and change? First, we hope that we shall continue to receive reader communications. Your responses will not only help us in our ongoing work, but will also be used in later editions.

Second, we hope that people will take some of the ideas and documents and change their degree of sophistication. If the ideas contained in this book are useful, they need to be written in styles suitable for experts in the field at one end of the spectrum and to kindergarten students at the other. This book is too non-technical for the former group and the language is too difficult for the latter.

Finally, we hope that people will transform *Teg's 1994* into other media: film, poetry, drama, drawings, etc. We are fully aware that some of the potentials for the human race which we have outlined in *Teg's 1994* could be better communicated in other media; each medium has its own potential and its own limitations. In such transformations, the story line of *Teg's* may not remain intact— or indeed be even perceivable. But what should remain is the essential stimulus toward thought about our common future, which was our main goal in writing this book.

——*R.T., J.M.S.*

APPENDIX

CONCEPT BASIS FOR THE MULTIHOGAN

All forms of the traditional Navajo hogan represent much more, culturally, than mere shelter. Some of the hogan uses are common to many cultures, some to few; in other cultures, the home is often used as an entertainment center, but rarely for ceremonial. The multi-concept, multi-use nature of the hogan suggested its use as a beginning model for the complex described in Part 1 of this book.

Described below are the concepts used in working out the Multihogan in material form. The relatively complex form, in comparison with the Navajo hogan, is paralleled by an increase in multi-use, based on multi-concept.

All housing performs certain functions, carried out well or inadequately, according to culture patterns and the degree of resources available. The dwelling acts as:

1. shelter
2. sleeping and resting facilities
3. provision for care of persons and possessions

An additional feature is nearly always included:

4. food preparation facilities

On the North American continent it is assumed that the above functions will be based on:
5. adequate light, heat, power, water, sewage, waste disposal installations

There are also a number of features generally held to be desirable, if not always possible:

6. space for resident-group socializing
7. space for resident-visitor socializing
8. privacy for residents
9. functional traffic patterns throughout the dwelling
10. provision for suitable accommodations for all ages and

states of persons, birth to senility implying a
flexible floor-plan in the living-space
11.   recreation and exercise facilities
12.   a satisfyingly high aesthetic level in appearance and
functioning

The Multihogan described in this book was based upon the twelve
dwelling concepts listed above. In addition to these, the function of
the Multihogan as a site for creative work and education necessi-
tated:

13.   education facilities and equipment
14.   hogan residents' work facilities and equipment
15.   guest work facilities

The functioning of the Multihogan as a creative / social center calls
for:

16.   ceremonial facilities, including "open house" celebrations
for non-residents

All structures built for use by people have a cultural / psychological basis, implicit or explicit. In the conceptualization of the Multihogan this basis was highly explicit, and played a predominant role
in the design. There are three aspects:

A.   Without, the structure exists *with* the environment,
not as pseudo-part of it.
B.   Within the Hogan, a feeling of balance between pull to
the outside and attraction to the center.
C.   A psychologically supportive atmosphere to all Hogan
residents, involving an awareness of choices, ongoing
organization, mental stimulation, integration into the
environment.

USE OF MULTIHOGAN DESIGN

There have been some inquiries as to the availability of the Multihogan plans. While building plans do exist, it would seem inappropriate to reproduce and distribute them generally.

The Multihogan design was based on the 16 concepts listed above.
While the first four functions are certain to be found in any structure

that a reader might build, all of the other 12 concepts represent the answers to personal or situational needs and would not necessarily be shared by readers. Each reader has a unique set of personal and situational needs which might be quite different from those used as a basis for the Multihogan. It is our suggestion that the reader interested in construction begin by listing personal aims and needs.

COMPUTER PRINT-OUT: COMPARISON OF THE HOGAN LODGE AND THE MULTIHOGAN

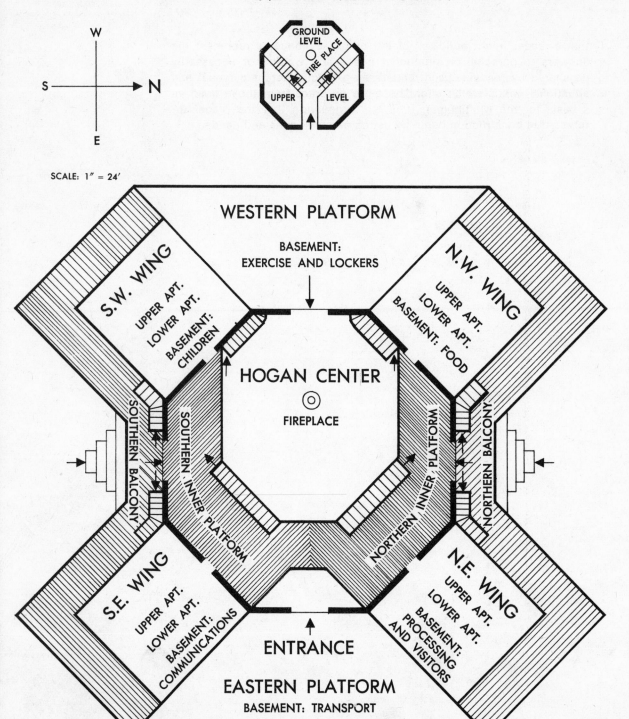

W
S — N
E

SCALE: 1" = 24'

GROUND LEVEL
FIRE PLACE
UPPER
LEVEL

WESTERN PLATFORM
BASEMENT: EXERCISE AND LOCKERS

S.W. WING
UPPER APT.
LOWER APT.
BASEMENT: CHILDREN

N.W. WING
UPPER APT.
LOWER APT.
BASEMENT: FOOD

HOGAN CENTER
FIREPLACE

SOUTHERN BALCONY

SOUTHERN INNER PLATFORM

NORTHERN INNER PLATFORM

NORTHERN BALCONY

S.E. WING
UPPER APT.
LOWER APT.
BASEMENT: COMMUNICATIONS

N.E. WING
UPPER APT.
LOWER APT.
BASEMENT: PROCESSING AND VISITORS

ENTRANCE

EASTERN PLATFORM
BASEMENT: TRANSPORT

COMPUTER PRINT-OUT: 3 RESIDENT APARTMENT LIVING ARRANGEMENTS

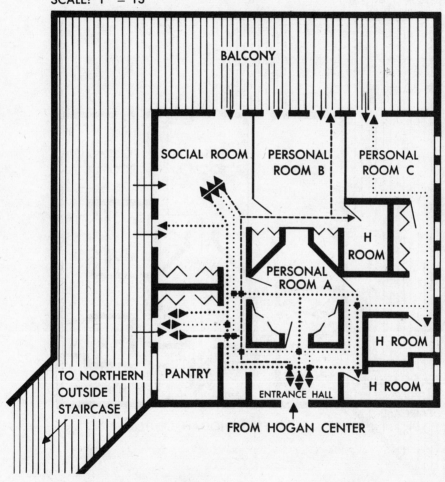

N.E. UPPER MIDDLE HOGAN

SCALE: 1" = 13'

BALCONY

SOCIAL ROOM

PERSONAL ROOM B

PERSONAL ROOM C

H ROOM

PERSONAL ROOM A

H ROOM

TO NORTHERN OUTSIDE STAIRCASE

PANTRY

H ROOM

ENTRANCE HALL

FROM HOGAN CENTER

KEY	SYSTEM TRAFFIC PATTERNS	SOCIO/PSYCHOLOGICAL INTERACTION PATTERNS
	(1) ⋮⋮⋮ PREDICTABLE PATHS	I ◆◆◆ ANTICIPATED MEETING
	(2) –●– SINGLE CROSS POINTS	II ◆◆ UNANTICIPATED MEETING
	(3) –●– MULTIPLE CROSS POINTS	

COMPUTER PRINT-OUT: 3 RESIDENT APARTMENT LIVING ARRANGEMENTS

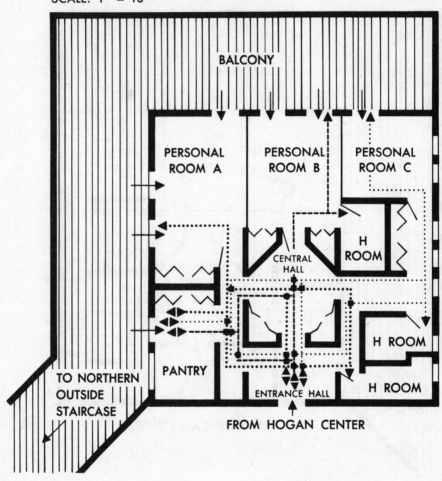

N.E. UPPER, NORTHERN HOGAN

SCALE: 1″ = 13′

BALCONY

PERSONAL ROOM A

PERSONAL ROOM B

PERSONAL ROOM C

H ROOM

CENTRAL HALL

PANTRY

H ROOM

TO NORTHERN OUTSIDE STAIRCASE

ENTRANCE HALL

H ROOM

FROM HOGAN CENTER

KEY

SYSTEM TRAFFIC PATTERNS

(1) PREDICTABLE PATHS

(2) SINGLE CROSS POINTS

(3) MULTIPLE CROSS POINTS

SOCIO/PSYCHOLOGICAL INTERACTION PATTERNS

I ANTICIPATED MEETING

II UNANTICIPATED MEETING

COMPARATIVE
APARTMENT DISTRIBUTION

NORTHERN HOGAN

(12 Adults)

S.E. Upper

3 Fellows (Men)

Room A, Personal room
    (Olaf)
Room B, Personal room
    (Mboya)
Room C, Personal room
    (Juan)

S.W. Upper

Board Member

Room A, Social room
Room B, Personal room
Room C

S.E. Lower

Facilitator

Room A, Social room
Room B, Study
Room C, Personal room

S.W. Lower

Empty

N.W. Upper

Facilitator (Luna)

Room A, Social room
Room B, Study
Room C, Personal room

N.E. Upper

3 Fellows (Women)

Room A, Personal room
     (Michiko)
Room B, Personal room
     (Teg)
Room C, Personal room
     (Mitzel)

N.W. Lower

General Facilitator
(Hassan and wife)

Room A, Hassan's study
Room B, Social room
Room C, Personal room

N.E. Lower

Facilitator

Room A, Social room
Room B, Study
Room C, Personal room

SOUTHERN HOGAN
(12 adults and 6 children)

S.E. Upper

2 Fellows (Men)

Room A, Personal room
        (Julius)
Room B, Personal room
        (Boris)
Room C,

N.W. Upper

2 Facilitators
(Husband and wife)

Room A, Husband's study
Room B, Wife's study
Room C, Personal room
Central Hall, Social room

S.W. Upper

Facilitator, wife, and child

Room A, Social room
Room B, Personal room
        (Boy, 2 years)
Room C, Personal room
        (Facilitator and
        wife)

N.E. Upper

Fellow and wife
(Pi-Lin and Lawrence)

Room A, Social room
Room B, Workroom
Room C, Personal room

S.E. Lower

2 Fellows (Women)

Room A, Personal room
    (Berthe)
Room B, Personal room
    (Marie)
Room C,

N.W. Lower

Empty

S.W. Lower

2 Children of S.W. Upper

Room A, Children's Social
    room
Room B, Personal room
    (Boy, 7 years)
Room C, Personal Room
    (Girl, 9 years)

N.E. Lower

Fellow, wife and 3 children

Room A, Social room
Room B, Personal room
    (Girl, 4 years
     Girl, 2½ years)
Room C, Personal room
    (Carla, Carlos,
     Boy, 6 months)

MIDDLE HOGAN
(14 adults and 7 children)

S.E. Upper

Couple and child

Room A, Social room
Room B, Personal room
     (Boy, 3 years)
Room C, Personal room
     (Husband and wife)

S.W. Upper

Couple and 3 children

Room A, Social room
Room B, Personal room
     (Boy, 6 years
      Boy, 5 years)
Room C, Personal Room
Ante-room, Girl, 9 months

S.E. Lower

2 children of S.E. Upper

Room A, Childrens' Social
     room
Room B, Personal room
     (Boy, 10 years)
Room C, Personal room
     (Girl, 8 years)

S.W. Lower

Couple and one child

S.W. Lower
Couple and one child
Room A, Social room
Room B, Personal room
     (Girl, 3 years)
Room C, Personal room
     (Husband and wife)

N.W. Upper	*N.E. Upper*
Empty	*3 men*
	Room A, Social room
	Room B, Personal room
	(One man)
	Central Hall, Personal room
	(One man)
	Room C, Personal room
	(One man)

N.W. Lower	*N.E. Lower*
Couple, Parents of S.E. Upper and S.W. Lower	3 Girls
Room A, Eating room	Room A, Personal room
Room B, Social room	(2 Girls)
Room C, Personal room	Room B, Social room
	Room C, Personal room
	(One Girl)
	Central Hall, Eating Room

VERY BRIEF BIBLIOGRAPHY

Heinlein, Robert. *Stranger in a Strange Land.* 1961. Paperback. New York: Berkeley Pub. Corp., 1968.

Herbert, Frank. *Dune.* 1965. Paperback. New York: Ace Books, 1965.

Two other volumes which employ a protagonist to describe a fundamentally changed world.

Postman, Neil, and Charles Weingartner. *The Soft Revolution.* Paperback. New York: Delta Books, 1971.

Translates non-competitive future orientation and styles into specific action possibilities and describes some steps which are already being taken.

Theobald, Robert. *An Alternative Future for America II.* 1970. Paperback. Chicago: The Swallow Press, Inc., 1970.

If you want to recommend the concepts of Teg's 1994 to another person, but you fear that the approach may not be useful for them, suggest they read *An Alternative Future for America II,* either first or instead.

Theobald, Robert. *The Economics of Abundance: A Non-Inflationary Future.* New York: Pitman Pub. Corp., 1970.

_____. *Habit and Habitat.* New York: Prentice-Hall, Inc., 1972.

Covers, in very different style and language, the issues raised by our growing understanding of system theory.